MW00655031

MALIEA'S HERO

BROTHERHOOD PROTECTORS HAWAII
BOOK FOUR

ELLE JAMES

TWISTED PAGE INC

ISBN EBOOK: 978-1-62695-559-2

ISBN PRINT: 978-1-62695-560-8

Dedicated to my sister who is the bravest person I know.
You're a badass, and I love you for it.
Elle James

AUTHOR'S NOTE

Enjoy other military books by Elle James

Brotherhood Protectors Hawaii

Kalea's Hero (#1)

Leilani's Hero (#2)

Kiana's Hero (#3)

Maliea's Hero (#4)

Emi's Hero (#5)

Sachie's Hero (#6)

Visit ellejames.com for more titles and release dates
Join her newsletter at
https://ellejames.com/contact/

MALIEA'S HERO

BROTHERHOOD PROTECTORS HAWAII
BOOK #4

New York Times & *USA Today*
Bestselling Author

ELLE JAMES

CHAPTER 1

Exhausted from a night dancing for a crowd of tourists at a luau, Maliea Kaleiopu swung by her apartment to shower and change into comfortable clothes before going to her friend Tish's place to pick up her daughter.

The night had been particularly hot, with high humidity and no breeze to cool them off between sets. Her skin was sticky with drying sweat. A quick glance in her visor mirror proved what she already knew. Between perspiration and humidity, her carefully applied makeup was sliding down her face.

She pulled up to the apartment she'd lived in for the past four years, wishing for the thousandth time she could afford a house with a yard.

Nani, her three-year-old daughter, had been asking for a dog. Apartments weren't conducive to owning dogs. Granted, many of their neighbors had dogs, but they had to walk them numerous times during the day and evening.

Since her husband's death, Maliea had had to work two jobs to make ends meet. Owning a house and caring for a pet didn't fit into her budget.

Taylor's income as a junior professor at the University of Hawaii hadn't paid a great deal. Between his income and her dancing, they'd managed to survive the high cost of living in Hawaii. He'd been doing what he'd loved, teaching Hawaiian history alongside Maliea's father, Professor John Hasegawa, the tenured history professor and head of the department. The two men had also spent time on archeological digs throughout the island chain, their true passion.

Maliea did what she loved, dancing in the traditional Hawaiian style for luaus, birthdays and other events.

They hadn't seen much of each other over the past year, with Taylor working days and Maliea working nights. They'd agreed it had to be that way until he was promoted, thus increasing his salary.

Maliea had noticed that she and Taylor had drifted further and further apart over the past year. Sex had been practically non-existent, not that she'd missed it. After nightly performances, she hadn't had the energy or desire.

She'd told herself they just had to weather their

situation a little longer. Once they had more money coming in, Maliea could back off working so many nights. Then they'd have more time together. They'd work on their relationship later.

It was always later.

Later hadn't come for Taylor.

He and Maliea's father had chartered a seaplane to fly to one of the smaller islands to investigate a clue regarding a lost treasure.

On their return, the plane had crashed into the ocean, killing all aboard.

In that one devastating crash, Maliea had lost her husband and her father. Though she and Taylor had drifted apart, she missed him. After all, they'd started out as friends. But the loss of her father had hit even harder. He'd been the rock in her life since her mother's death from cancer. She had always counted on him when she'd needed advice, a safety net or just a hug. She still found it hard to breathe.

Only a couple of weeks had passed since their deaths. Maliea needed to go to Taylor's and her father's offices at the university to collect their personal effects. She also needed to go to her father's apartment and sort through his belongings.

She just hadn't had the heart to do it. Not yet. The wounds on her heart were still raw.

Maybe tomorrow. She had a few days off between gigs. She wouldn't need the expense of a babysitter because she could take Nani with her.

She parked in the lot adjacent to her apartment complex, got out and grabbed the gym bag she carried to and from performances. It contained makeup, hair products and other things she needed. For the larger performances, the dance troupe provided the costumes and managed their transportation and cleaning. Thank goodness.

With her key in hand, Maliea carried the gym bag up the steps and across the landing to her apartment. When she went to stick the key in the lock, the door pushed open. That's when she noticed the splintered door jamb.

Her pulse leaped into hyper-drive. She backed away from the door and spun, running back the way she'd come. When she reached her car, she jumped in, locked the doors and rested her hands on the steering wheel while her heart raced so fast she could barely breathe.

She pulled her cell phone out of her purse and hit 911 as she stared up at the landing outside her door, fully expecting to see someone emerge from her apartment.

When a woman's voice answered and asked, "What's your emergency?" Maliea almost sobbed.

She swallowed hard and blurted, "Someone broke into my apartment."

"Are you inside the apartment now?" the dispatcher asked.

"No." Maliea's hand shook as she held the phone to her ear.

"Are you in a safe place?"

"I'm in my car, outside the building," Maliea said. "Doors are locked."

"Is the intruder still in your apartment?"

Maliea said. "I-I don't know. I'd just come home from work. When I started to unlock the door, I noticed it was already open. I-I ran."

"Good," the woman said, her tone steady, smooth and calming. "Don't try to go into the apartment. I have a unit en route to your location, ETA five minutes. You can stay on the phone with me until they arrive."

"Thank you," Maliea said, clutching the phone like a lifeline. While Maliea waited, the woman on the other end of the line talked with her, asking her questions about her life, what she did for a living and expressed interest when Maliea said she was a Hawaiian dancer. Time passed quickly, and Maliea's heartbeat slowed closer to normal.

In under five minutes, a Honolulu Police car arrived in the apartment's parking lot, its lights flashing.

"They're here," Maliea announced to the woman who'd stayed on the line with her. "Thank you for staying with me."

"My pleasure," the woman said and ended the call.

When Maliea started to get out of her car, the police officer held up a hand and shook his head. "Let us check it out first." He and his partner climbed the stairs and paused outside her door, standing on either side, their weapons drawn. Then, one of the officers slipped inside, followed by the other.

Moments later, an officer appeared in the doorway and motioned for Maliea to come up.

Her pulse quickening again, she climbed the stairs, crossed the landing and met the officer at the door.

"Whoever broke in is gone," he said. "But I'm sorry to say, he left a mess. You'll need to go through everything and let us know what's missing. Be careful not to touch or disturb anything. We'll have someone dust for prints."

Maliea entered, her breath catching.

The small apartment was never truly pristine with a three-year-old living there. But this...

She shook her head.

In the living room, the hand-me-down sofa her father had given them lay on its back, the cushions thrown or ripped as if someone had slashed them with a knife. Drawers had been pulled from the end tables and lay in pieces as if someone had smashed them.

Maliea stepped close to the tiny kitchen, where every drawer had been dumped on the floor and the pantry emptied, with cereal scattered across every surface. Shelves were empty, the contents of her canisters strewn across every surface. Flour, sugar and pasta lay on the floor in a thick layer.

The officer reached out to block her entry into the kitchen. He nodded toward the flour on the floor. "Don't disturb the footprints."

Maliea nodded and continued through the living room.

The basket of Nani's toys lay upside down, toys flung in a broad circle. Her favorite stuffed bear was missing its head, the stuffing pulled from its body.

Acid roiled in the pit of Maliea's belly. Who would do such a thing? Ripping a child's toy to shreds seemed so...violent.

Leaving everything where it was, Maliea moved slowly down the hall. The photos she'd hung in inexpensive frames had been ripped from the wall, the frames destroyed, the photos left behind crumpled. The picture of her father holding Nani two months ago lay torn and wrinkled. Seeing it like that was like a sucker punch to her belly. Maliea automatically bent to pick it up. She caught herself before her fingers touched the paper.

Tears welled in her eyes. Her heart squeezed hard in her chest as she pushed past the damaged photos and frames to enter Nani's bedroom with the twin-sized bed Maliea had decorated with a fluffy pink comforter and matching curtains.

The curtains had been ripped from the wall, and the bent rod hung askew from one side. The pink comforter, torn down the middle, lay in a wad beside the mattress on the floor. Again, as if someone had taken a knife to the bed, the fitted sheet and mattress had been ripped down the middle.

As she stared at the savaged mattress, all Maliea could think was that if they had been home when the intruder had made his entrance...

Her stomach tightened, and bile rose up her throat. With nothing of value to others in her daughter's room, Maliea moved on to her own.

She didn't own fancy jewelry except for the diamond necklace her father had given her mother on their tenth anniversary. Her mother had given it to Maliea in the last days of her fight against cancer.

As she entered her bedroom, Maliea immediately crossed the room to her dresser. The top right drawer had held her keepsakes and the jewel box containing the necklace. The drawer was gone, the contents spread across the floor.

Maliea looked past her ripped mattress and shredded comforter, searching for the box containing the necklace.

Despite the officer's adamance about not

disturbing anything, Maliea dug through the clothes and documents until she found the black velvet box. When she opened it and found the diamond necklace nestled against the velvet interior, tears filled her eyes and slipped down her cheeks.

She stood, clutching the box in her hands, shaking her head as she looked around the room.

Though the intruder had destroyed items of great emotional value to Maliea and Nani, he hadn't taken the only thing of any value to anyone else.

"Is anything missing that you can tell?" the officer asked from the doorway.

She shook her head. "Would it be all right if I took some clothes for me and my daughter?"

The man nodded. "Take what you need. And you might want to find somewhere else to stay for the night."

She snorted softly. Maliea would have to find somewhere else to stay for a while. She couldn't bring Nani back to this disaster. She'd be traumatized.

After giving her information to the officer and gathering a trash bag full of clothes and toiletries for herself and Nani, Maliea left the apartment, climbed into her car and drove to Tish's apartment, sick inside, the feeling of having had her home violated making her skin crawl. Their safe haven was no longer safe. Where else could they go?

Tish Jenkins already had a new roommate, Solange, since her old roommate, Meredith Smith, had moved in with her half-sister, Tina. Tish and Solange were models who worked in an escort agency between modeling assignments.

Solange didn't mind when Tish watched Nani, but their apartment was too small to take on another woman, especially one with a small child.

Maliea would have to find temporary lodging for herself and Nani, at least until she could clean up the mess and find furniture to replace what had been destroyed.

Her fingers tightened around the steering wheel. She had no savings, and her father's estate was in probate. Living paycheck to paycheck wasn't conducive to affording a hotel for an extended period or even one night. Not at Honolulu prices.

The important thing for her to remember was that she and Nani were unharmed. Until the police found the person responsible, Maliea wouldn't feel safe in her apartment. If he could get in so easily the first time, he could do it again. If the intruder came back, he might catch them at home.

She couldn't risk it. Not when her daughter's life was at stake.

Maliea parked outside Tish's apartment building, gathered her trash bag of belongings and climbed the stairs to Tish's apartment, looking over her shoulder the entire way.

When Tish opened the door, she stared at Maliea and the trash bag. "Mal? Are you okay?"

Maliea shook her head, holding it together by a thread. She glanced over Tish's shoulder. "Where's Nani?"

"Asleep on my bed." Tish stepped aside and motioned for Maliea to enter the apartment. She reached for the trash bag and dragged it across the threshold.

Once Maliea was inside, Tish closed and locked the door. "What's happened? Why do you look like you're about to fall apart?"

Tears welled in Maliea's eyes. "Someone broke into..." a sob rose in her throat, choking off her words, "...my apartment."

"Oh my god, Mal, are you okay?" Tish pulled Maliea into her arms, her own body shaking. "Did he hurt you? Did you call the police? What the hell?"

Maliea let the tears she'd held back flow now that she was in the relative safety of her friend's arms. After a minute, she sniffed and pulled back, wiping the moisture from her face. "I'm okay. Just shaken. I wasn't there when it happened. Whoever did it came through while I was at work." She shook her head. "Oh, Tish, you should see the mess he left. I don't think he left anything untouched. It looks like a war zone."

Tish hooked Maliea's arm and led her into the living room to the sofa. "Sit. I'm going to get you a drink, then you can tell me everything."

Maliea sank onto the sofa, snatched a tissue from a box on the end table and blew her nose.

Moments later, Tish appeared with two wine glasses and a bottle of cabernet sauvignon. "Sweetie, spill while I pour." She sat beside Maliea and poured two glasses of wine.

Maliea told her how she'd arrived at her apartment and found the door opened and the door jamb busted.

Tish's face blanched. "You didn't go in, did you?"

Maliea shook her head. "I ran back to my car and called the police. It wasn't until they cleared the apartment that I went in. The intruder was already gone."

"Thank God," Tish touched her arm. "I'm so glad he didn't break in while you and Nani were there."

Maliea hugged Tish. "I'm sorry. I shouldn't be unloading on you. Not after what you went through."

Tish hugged her with one arm, careful not to spill the wine in her other hand. "Honey, I'm fine. I survived. That's what counts. You don't have to tiptoe around me."

"Tish, you were in a coma." Maliea shook her head. "You nearly died."

"But I didn't." Tish lifted her chin. "I took self-defense classes. I can kick ass now. And I'm stronger for having gone through the attack." She sat back and stared into Maliea's face. "The question here is why someone would target your apartment, or you, for that matter?"

Maliea shook her head. "I don't know. The only thing I own of value is the diamond necklace my mother left me. The intruder didn't take it. As far as I can tell, he didn't take anything."

Tish's brow furrowed. "Then why destroy your apartment?"

Maliea pinched the bridge of her nose. "I don't know. What I do know is that I can't go back to my apartment with Nani. If she saw it the way it is, she'd be upset. And I don't trust that whoever ransacked it won't come back." She grimaced. "I know it's a lot to ask after you kept Nani entertained all evening, but would you mind if we stayed the night? Nani can sleep on the couch. I don't mind sleeping on the floor."

Tish frowned. "Mal, you know you're welcome here. Solange and I love our little Nani to pieces."

Maliea smiled, tears welling in her eyes. "I don't know what I'd do without you and Solange. You're my only family."

Tish wrapped her arms around Maliea and held

her tight. "Damn right. And don't you forget that we're family."

Maliea leaned into her friend...the sister she'd always wished she had. "Thank you."

Tish snorted. "For what? Doing the right thing?"

Maliea leaned back and brushed the moisture from her cheeks. "For being you." Another thought had her frowning again. "If the intruder is after me, do you think he'll look for me here?" Her frown deepened. "The last thing I want is to bring trouble to you and Solange. Maybe we should find a hotel for the night."

"No way," Tish said. "You're staying here. We can push a dresser in front of the door if it makes you feel better. You're not taking my Nani to a hotel where you have no one to protect both of you."

"But—"

"No buts," Tish said. "Now, since Nani is already asleep in my bed, she can stay there. You can sleep with her. I'll sleep on the couch. I'd offer Solange's room, but she'll be back around midnight. She's on an escort gig."

Maliea lifted her chin. "I can be just as stubborn as you. I won't take your bed or Solange's. Nani's comfortable with you and has slept with you before. You two take the bed; I'll sleep on the couch. Tomorrow, we'll figure out something else."

"Okay, you don't have to twist my arm," Tish

said with a grin. "Nani and I will be on the bed. I'll get a blanket and pillow for you." She disappeared into the bedroom.

Maliea followed.

While Tish pulled a blanket out of the closet, Maliea bent over her sleeping daughter and brushed a kiss across her forehead. Her heart swelled in her chest. Her marriage might not have been great, but she wouldn't have traded it for anything. Nani was the result of their union. She was everything to Maliea.

Her gut clenched at the thought of an intruder breaking into her apartment while they were there. Maliea hadn't taken the self-defense classes like Tish, and she didn't have a weapon she could use to defend them.

Maliea prayed the police would find the intruder and put him in jail. The odds of them catching a random intruder were probably low. In the meantime, she couldn't impose on Tish and Solange for long.

Maliea tucked the blanket around her daughter and straightened.

Tish tipped her head toward the living room, her arms full of a blanket and a pillow.

Maliea followed her out of the bedroom and pulled the door almost all the way closed behind them.

Tish spread the blanket on the couch and laid

the pillow on one end. "Is there anything else you need for the night?"

Maliea's lips twisted. "Peace of mind?"

Tish hugged her. "That will take time. I'd stay up with you a little longer, but I have an early morning shoot. I need my beauty sleep."

"Of course," Maliea said, a stab of guilt hitting her square in the chest. As a model, Tish had to be fresh and ready to go. "Don't let me keep you up."

Tish tilted her head, her brow creased. "What are your plans for tomorrow?"

"I'm off for the next two days. I'd planned to go by Taylor's office at the university to gather his personal belongings. If I'm up to it, I'll stop by my father's office next. I've put it off long enough."

Tish sighed. "I can only imagine how hard it's been. To lose your father and your husband at the same time is horrible."

Maliea sighed. "It's not like Taylor and I had the best relationship. We never saw each other."

"Yeah. I know you two were struggling with opposing shifts." Tish folded her arms over her chest. "I remember there were nights you had off, but he worked late. He could've tried harder."

"I'm sad we didn't have time to work things out." Maliea sniffed. "But losing my dad..." She bit down on her lip to keep it from trembling. "I'm heartbroken. He was my rock. I could handle anything, knowing he was always there for me and Nani."

"I'm so sorry." Tish started toward her, arms outstretched.

Maliea held up a hand. "I'll be okay. You need your sleep."

Tish stopped. "Are you sure?"

Maliea squared her shoulders. "I have to be. For Nani's sake, if not for mine." She dropped onto the couch. "Goodnight, Tish. Thanks for everything."

Tish remained where she was standing. "The shoot shouldn't take longer than a few hours. If you wait until then, I can go with you to the university."

"I can do it on my own," Maliea said.

"But you don't have to," Tish said. "Wait. Let me come with you—especially when you go to your father's office."

Maliea hesitated, not wanting to burden her friend any more than she had.

"You know you want me there," Tish said with a smile. "You're waiting, and I'm going with you. What about Nani? Is she coming, too?"

Maliea shook her head. "She was looking forward to attending the Mother's Day Out program tomorrow. She has little friends she likes playing with there. Do you think she'll be safe?"

Tish's eyes narrowed. "We don't know what the intruder was after at your apartment. Since he trashed it, I'd think he was looking for some*thing*, not some*one*. For all you know, it was a random act."

"The Mother's Day Out program is next door to a branch of the Honolulu Police Department. They have strict rules for drop-off and pick-up. I can also tell them to be extra wary." Maliea sighed. "Or I could take her with me to the university. She'll be disappointed, but I'll feel better having her in sight."

"Then it's settled," Tish said. "You're waiting for me, and Nani's coming with us." She turned and walked toward the bedroom. "Now, I'm going for some beauty sleep, or they'll fire me before we start tomorrow morning. Don't forget...Solange should be in around midnight."

"I won't forget," Maliea said.

Tish entered the bedroom, leaving the door wide open.

For a long time, Maliea lay on the couch, staring up at the low ceiling of the apartment, wondering what to do next. She couldn't take Nani back to the apartment after an intruder had compromised their supposedly safe haven.

Where else could they go until the burglar was caught? She didn't have spare cash or a relative to visit. Just Tish and Solange.

Close to midnight, Maliea's thoughts finally calmed enough to let her close her eyes.

She'd just drifted off to sleep when a sound jerked her awake. A quick glance at the clock on her cell phone confirmed it was a few minutes shy of midnight.

Maliea rose from the couch and walked barefoot to the door to peer through the peephole.

The hallway in front of the door was empty. The sound she'd heard happened again.

Maliea turned to the window overlooking the parking lot below. She lifted a slat and stared down at the parking lot where she'd left her car, expecting to see Solange any moment.

Nothing moved in the parking lot full of cars. Solange had yet to arrive.

As Maliea dropped the slat, a movement caught her attention. She lifted the blind slat again and stared down at a shadowy figure wearing what looked like a black ski mask. He held something in his hand, sliding it along the passenger side window of a car.

Maliea's pulse leaped. "That's my car," she whispered.

The person who was standing beside her vehicle opened the door.

Maliea gasped. "Holy shit, he unlocked the door."

At that moment, another vehicle turned into the parking lot, headlights glancing off the side of Maliea's car. The man who'd opened her car door closed it and ducked down beside her car.

The vehicle with the headlights pulled into the

parking space beside Maliea's car. At that moment, she recognized the red Jeep Solange had found on a used car lot.

With her pulse banging through her veins, Maliea ran for Tish's bedroom, shook her friend awake and whispered, "Call 911. Someone is breaking into my car, and Solange just drove up."

Tish sat up, blinking sleep from her eyes. "Wait...what?"

Maliea didn't have time to explain. "Call 911." She spun and ran for the apartment door, unsure what she should do, but she couldn't let the man breaking into her car hurt Solange.

As Maliea passed through Tish's apartment, she searched for something to use as a weapon, settling on an umbrella leaning against the wall by the door. She snagged the curved handle, unlocked the door and ran out into the hallway, down the stairs and out into the parking lot, fired by rage burning inside. Deep down, she knew. This was the same person who'd ravaged her apartment.

"You might have destroyed my home," she muttered, "but by damned, you're not going to hurt my friend!"

CHAPTER 2

Solange had just pushed open the door to her vehicle when Maliea ran out into the parking lot, barefoot and wielding the umbrella like a baseball bat, screaming like a banshee.

Solange stared at her like she'd completely lost her mind.

"Solange," Maliea yelled, "stay in your car!" She raced around her friend's Jeep and the front of her four-door black sedan to the passenger side, ready to pound the attacker with the wooden handle of the umbrella.

The space between her car and the next was empty.

As Maliea started to bend to glance beneath her car, a hand snaked out, grabbed her ankle and yanked hard.

Maliea lost her balance and fell back against the

next car, hitting her head hard as she crashed to the ground. The umbrella flew through the air and clattered against the pavement.

The hand on her ankle tightened, pulling her leg beneath the sedan's chassis.

Her head spinning, Maliea fought to stay conscious. If this man killed her, he might go after Solange next. Maliea couldn't let that happen. She had to hold on. Had to fight him until the police came.

Half aware and on the brink of passing out, Maliea cocked her free leg and kicked against the hand holding onto her ankle. She had to get free, find her umbrella and hit the bastard as hard as she could. Too stunned to realize how insane that sounded, she kicked again, her feeble attempts having little effect on the man's grip.

The sound of a siren penetrated the black fog, threatening to pull Maliea under.

Hope swelled in her chest, even as the fog thickened.

The siren's blare grew louder.

Maliea kicked again. Though her head throbbed, the gray haze of semiconsciousness began clearing with each passing second.

The grip on her ankle released. The shadowy figure beneath her car faded into the darkness.

"Maliea!" Solange's voice called out.

Fighting through a massive headache, Maliea

rolled over and pushed up onto her hands and knees.

"Maliea!" Solange rounded the front of the car, holding a tire iron over her head, ready to strike.

"Be careful," Maliea said. "He was under my car." She reached for the umbrella and poked at the darkness beneath her vehicle. "Need a goddamn flashlight."

A small light blinked on over Maliea's shoulder. Solange handed her a cell phone with the flashlight app on.

Maliea shined the light beneath her car. The man was gone. She pushed to her feet, swayed, braced her hand on the car next to her and looked around. Nothing moved. Not a single shadow moved among the other parked vehicles.

Moments later, flashing lights bounced off the brick buildings as a police car pulled into the parking lot and stopped close to Maliea and Solange. The officer leaped out, gun drawn, but remained behind the relative shield his door provided. "Hands in the air," he called out.

Solange dropped the tire iron. It clattered against the pavement as she raised both hands into the air.

Maliea followed suit, letting go of the umbrella and raising her hands. The situation was so ridiculous, or she was teetering on the verge of hysteria, that she had the sudden urge to laugh. She'd been attacked, but the officer was holding a gun on her, not her attacker. How ironic was that?

"Officer," Maliea called out, "We're not the people breaking into my car. A man dressed in black with a black ski mask is the one you should be looking for before he gets away."

The policeman ignored her comment. "I need you both to step away from the vehicle," he said.

Another patrol car roared into the apartment complex parking lot and skidded to a stop, lights flashing, siren screaming. The officer in that car leaped out just like the other and stood behind the door with his gun drawn.

"Good grief," Solange muttered as she and Maliea stepped away from the car.

Once they were in the open and the officer could ascertain they were not armed, he let them drop their arms. The two officers relaxed, switched off their flashing lights and closed the distance between them.

While the initial officer questioned them, the second man searched the parking lot.

Maliea snorted. They wouldn't find the attacker. He was long gone—probably as soon as he heard the sirens wailing toward them.

After ten more minutes, with them giving their statements, Maliea and Solange were allowed to go up to the apartment.

Tish opened the door before Maliea could reach

for the handle. "Nani is still sleeping, sirens and all. What happened? Are you all right? I saw you go down and then I couldn't see you at all." She gripped Maliea's arms and stared into her face. "I was so worried and wanted to come down to help, but—"

"You had to stay with Nani," Maliea finished. "You did the right thing. Solange came to my rescue like a Valkyrie with her tire iron." Maliea grinned.

Solange shrugged. "It was the only weapon I could find. Speaking of which, remind me to put it back in my Jeep."

"But you went down fast," Tish said. "What happened?"

Maliea rubbed the back of her head. "The guy was hiding under my car. He grabbed my ankle, yanked me down and tried to drag me under the chassis. If not for Solange and the police coming at that moment, I don't know what would have happened." Maliea hugged Solange. "Thank you."

"Oh, Maliea, I was so scared." Solange hugged her so tightly that Maliea could barely breathe.

"Well, that does it." Tish crossed her arms over her chest. "I don't like where this is headed. I think you need more help than we can give."

Maliea stepped away from Solange. "I know. I need to find another place to stay. If that man comes back, you ladies will be at risk, as well." She shook her head. "I couldn't live with myself if something happened to you because of me."

"Nonsense," Tish said. "You're staying tonight. But tomorrow, we're getting more help—professional help to protect you and Nani. I know just who to call." Her gaze went to Solange.

Solange's eyes widened along with a smile. "Brotherhood Protectors? Or one in particular?"

Tish gave a brief nod. "One in particular. I'll send you to the man who protected me while I was in a coma. He said that if I ever needed help again, I should let him know. I think you need help."

"As much as I'd like the help," Maliea said, "I can't afford to pay for it. And he was talking to you, not me."

"From what Kiana said, money's never a problem with the Brotherhood Protectors. Hank Patterson, the founder, and his wife, Sadie McClain, fund the project when needed to ensure people who need it most have the protection they require, regardless of their ability to pay. You need help. I think they'll provide it. If not Reid, then one of the other guys who work for the Brotherhood Protectors."

Maliea chewed on her bottom lip. "Are you sure? I'd hate to accept help and get a bill later that I have no way of paying. I can barely keep up with my rent, utilities and groceries since Taylor died."

Solange touched her arm. "Trust her. They can

help. Not only did they protect Tish, but they also saved Kiana's life when she was targeted by the man who wanted her for body parts."

Tish nodded. "At least talk to Reid. He'll give you all the information you'll need to decide."

Reluctant to accept charity, Maliea was too tired to think of any alternatives. "Okay. I'll talk with him. Does he have another name besides Reid? And what's his background? What makes him someone who can provide the protection Nani and I need?"

Tish grinned. "Reid Bennett is an ex-Navy SEAL, highly trained in combat and self-defense with years of experience in special operations. He has performed combat missions, rescued people in dangerous situations and provided protection for important dignitaries. The guy knows his stuff."

"Why would he want to help me?" Maliea asked. "It's not like I'm an important dignitary."

"Sweetie, you're important to me," Tish said. "Besides, he's not in the Navy anymore. He works with the Brotherhood Protectors, utilizing some of that training to protect civilians. In fact, he and two other members of his team are currently working a job out at the Kualoa Ranch, providing security to a movie production company."

"Then he's already on assignment," Maliea said. "He won't have time for me and Nani."

"Maybe not, but he'll get in touch with his boss,

and they'll assign another protector to you and Nani." Tish crossed to the table by the door where she'd left her purse and pulled out her cell phone. "I have his phone number and the address where he's staying. Since the production company will be there for several weeks, he rented a small cabin."

Maliea pushed a hand through her hair, tired to the bone from her earlier performance and everything else that had happened since she'd arrived at her apartment and Tish's. "It all seems so intense."

"I can take you out to him tomorrow, but not until after I get back from my early morning shoot. It'll be noon before I can take you." Tish frowned.

Solange held up a hand. "I'd take her, but I'm flying out early tomorrow for that job on Maui. It's my first commercial. I hate to bail on them when they only have two days to shoot it."

"No." Tish tapped a finger to her chin. "You have to go. It's too big an opportunity to pass up. No, I'll call and tell the photographer I can't do tomorrow."

"But you've been waiting for good weather to get those morning shots. Tomorrow is supposed to be perfect," Solange said.

"We can't leave Maliea and Nani alone."

Maliea held up a hand. "Neither one of you is going to cancel anything. I know how hard it is for you to get paying modeling or acting work. I won't be the one to sabotage your careers. I can drive out to meet with this Reid guy with Nani."

"That guy found your car here," Tish said. "He might have tagged it with a tracking device. He could follow you out to Kualoa Ranch."

"She can take my Jeep," Solange offered. "I can Uber to the airport."

Tish's frown deepened. "Your bright red Jeep?" She shook her head. "It's like waving a flag in front of every bull in the arena. She needs something more subdued, like every other car in the parking lot." Her lips twisted. "She needs my hunk of junk gray sedan."

"I can take an Uber out there," Maliea offered, wondering where she'd get the money to pay for a ride like that out to the Kualoa Ranch.

"No," Tish said. "What if this guy showed up as your Uber driver? I wouldn't trust anyone you don't know."

"But you want me to trust your Reid Bennet?" Maliea asked. "I don't know him."

"But I do."

"And so do I," Solange said. "He's the real deal."

"You can trust him with your life," Tish said. "And more importantly, with Nani's life."

"You and Nani can't stay here alone," Solange said. "That guy knows you're here."

"She's right," Tish said. "I can take your car. You can take mine, and he won't know where you went."

"That puts you at risk," Maliea said. "He could come after you thinking it's me."

Tish's eyes narrowed. "Let the bastard try. I'll kick his ass."

"Oh, Tish," Maliea shook her head. "I don't want you hurt."

"Look," Tish said. "My shoot is on the beach. Very few people will be parked out there that early. If it makes you feel better, I'll make sure someone walks me to the car to be safe. We can leave at the same time to confuse the guy. By the time he figures out you're not driving your car, he will have missed his opportunity to follow you, and you'll be on the other side of Oahu by then." A grin spread across her face. "Clever, huh?"

"All three of us will leave early," Solange said. "That's one more car to add to the mix. We can leave the apartment wearing sunglasses and hats. He'll never guess who's who."

"But I'll have Nani," Maliea said.

Both Solange and Tish's shoulders sagged.

"Right." Tish tapped a finger to her chin. "Nani's small enough..." Her eyes narrowed even further as she looked across at Solange. "Do you still have those big beach bags you, Kiana and I bought on sale last year?"

Solange nodded. "Yes. It's in the hall closet with yours."

Tish's mouth curved. "I'll bet Kiana's is in there

as well. I don't think she took it when she moved to Maui." Tish hurried to the hall closet, returned a moment later carrying three large canvas beach totes and dumped their contents on the floor.

Snorkels, fins and masks spilled out of each.

"We liked them because they were big enough to carry all our snorkeling equipment, including fins." Tish held the bag open. "Do you think Nani will fit in one of these?"

Maliea stared down into the bag, imagining little Nani curled into the bottom. "I suppose."

"Solange, do you still have your ex's bowling ball?" Tish asked.

Solange grinned. "I do. I told him I couldn't find it, but then I discovered it under my gym bag." She rolled her eyes toward the corner of the room. "I don't know how it got there." Her grin twisted into a frown. "I think he loved his bowling ball more than me. Anyway, I haven't told him I found it. Do you want me to put it in one of the bags?"

Tish nodded. "Along with some padding like towels or clothes. I can toss in my twenty-five-pound kettlebell in the bottom of mine, along with a pillow or towels. That way, all three of us will have matching bags, be disguised, and walk out of here at the same time. If someone is stalking Maliea, they won't know which one of us she is." She clapped her hands together.

"Sounds complicated," Maliea worried.

"It'll work," Tish said. "Now, I really have to get some sleep, or I'll lose this job because of the circles beneath my eyes."

"They wouldn't dare fire you," Maliea said. "You're beautiful no matter how much sleep you get."

"Thank you," Tish said with a smile. "I love you, too. Set your alarms for five thirty. We'll bug out at six. In the morning, I'll text Reid, letting him know you're coming early. If anything, you can camp out in his cabin while he's at his job on the ranch. You're safer there than here."

"Especially if your stalker doesn't know where you are," Solange added. "Night, ladies."

Tish grabbed a chair from the small dinette table, shoved it under the apartment doorknob, checked the deadbolt and nodded. "That should slow anyone down." She glanced at Maliea. "If you're nervous about sleeping out here on the couch, you can have my room with Nani. Last chance to change your mind."

Maliea shook her head. "No. You need your beauty sleep. I don't. Besides, I doubt I'll sleep at all. Too much has happened. It's better that I stay out here so I don't disturb you or Nani."

"Suit yourself," Tish said. "See you in the morning." She entered her bedroom and closed the door halfway, leaving it open enough that Maliea could listen for her daughter should she wake in the night.

Maliea turned off all the lights in the living room. A night light in the kitchenette cast enough of a glow she could get around without bumping into things. Barefooted, she paced the length of the living room several times, trying hard to resist peeking out the window at the parking lot below.

Would the man come back and try to break into her car? If so, what was he after? Maybe he wasn't interested in her or Nani at all. He could have been looking for anything of value she might have left in the vehicle. Not that she had anything of any value in her car or her apartment—except the diamond necklace that wasn't worth enough to break into an apartment for.

Unable to resist, Maliea pushed a slat of the blinds up and stared down at the parking lot and her car.

Nothing stirred.

Tish would need to make sure no one was in her car when she got into it the next morning. The guy had unlocked the door once. He could do it again. In fact, he could slip in, wait until whoever was driving it got in behind the wheel and—

Maliea dropped the slat and stepped away from the window. She'd make sure no one was hiding in her car the next morning before anyone got in it.

Tish was her friend. By pretending to be Maliea, she was taking a big risk.

What choice did Maliea have? The police would do nothing to protect her and Nani. How could they? They were always short-handed. No one had blatantly attacked them yet.

Was she being overly cautious?

Her thoughts went to her beautiful three-year-old daughter. She could never be too cautious where Nani was concerned. Maliea had already lost so much with the deaths of her husband and father. She wouldn't survive if she lost Nani. That little girl was her world. Tish's Reid had better be all she painted him to be.

If he wasn't?

Hell, she didn't know what else to do.

Well after midnight, Maliea lay on the couch and stared up at the ceiling, her mind still spinning out of control with all the worst-case scenarios.

She wasn't sure who was behind the attacks, but she couldn't risk Nani's life by refusing help.

Maliea closed her eyes. "Please, Mr. Bennett, be all Tish says you are," she whispered softly.

CHAPTER 3

REID WAS ALREADY on the set at Kualoa Ranch when he received the text from Tish.

Tish: My friend is in trouble. Needs a place to stay and a protector. Sending my friend your way early this morning. Please help.

With a frown, he texted Tish back.

Reid: Already at the set. Tell him there's a key under the mat on the back porch. He can make himself at home until I get back.

Reid glanced up from his cell phone at the movie crew setting up cameras in the valley below. They'd started early to beat the forecasted rain that was predicted to move in after eleven that morning.

His position was high above the actual movie set as a lookout for any trouble or overzealous fans who might try to sneak in on four-wheelers or horses.

Normally, Kualoa Ranch offered adventure tours to tourists who wanted to see the old WWII bunkers built into the sides of the hills or to see where movies like *Jurassic Park* and *King Kong* had been filmed.

The production company had reserved the ranch for two weeks to record the sequences they needed. They'd made good time the first week and would wrap up that morning if the weather held off long enough to get good footage.

Thus far, Reid and his team had had very few problems to deal with. They'd steered a group of teens away who'd heard Jason Momoa was one of the movie stars on location at the ranch.

Rex Johnson, dressed in a black polo shirt, black trousers and mirrored sunglasses, had run interference on that one. Looking like a man from the set of *Men in Black*, he'd informed them that Momoa wasn't one of the stars. He was working on a movie in the Bahamas for the next two months and wouldn't be in Hawaii anytime soon. He'd also informed them that the ranch was closed until after the movie crew left. Of all of them, Rex was the most likely to know the truth of Momoa's whereabouts, having come from a wealthy family out of LA. He'd gone to high school with some of the current movie stars who had a legacy of family members in film.

A stray cow had wandered onto the set at one point. Logan Atkins, Reid's team member with the most experience with cattle, had shooed the bovine out of the scene and back through the gate someone had left open.

All in all, it had been an easy assignment. One Logan and Rex could have handled without Reid. He could miss a few hours on the set and go check out the friend Tish had sent his way.

He spoke into his headset, "Rex, Logan, Sitrep?"

"Watching grass grow here," Rex responded.

"Was kind of hoping a rogue cow would find his way through the fence about now," Logan muttered.

"Bored?" Reid asked.

"Understatement," Rex said. "I'll be glad when the chase scene comes close to my position."

"All's quiet on the Hawaiian front," Logan concluded. "Why? What's up?"

"I got a text from Tish."

"The hot model?" Logan asked.

"The one you babysat while she was in a coma?" Rex clarified.

"That's the one," Reid said.

"Does she need a bodyguard for a beach photo shoot?" Logan continued. "I could sacrifice my position on a movie set to keep an eye on women modeling bikinis on the beach."

"Sorry, Logan," Reid said. "She has a friend who needs help."

"Another model, like Kiana?" Rex asked.

"She didn't say," Reid said. "I'm going to meet him at my cabin."

"Him?" Logan sighed. "I was hoping for female models in bikinis. Yeah, you go, Reid. I might as well stick to the movie set. At least I hear the word *Action*, even if I'm not getting any."

"What are you talking about?" Rex said. "Weren't you chatting up the cute blonde at the Burger Bar in town last night? Did she shoot you down?"

"Crashed and burned, man," Logan said. "Crashed and burned."

Rex chuckled. "Probably recognized you as the player you are."

"Bite me. Besides, we weren't talking about me," Logan groused. "Reid has a date with a dude. Talk about that."

"I don't have a date. I'm going to meet with a potential client. Can I trust you two to be serious and keep an eye on things here?"

"You bet," Rex said. "We've got things under control here. Let us know if it turns into an assignment. We'll be wrapping up here soon."

"Yeah. It would be nice to know what's next," Logan seconded.

"I'll let you know," Reid promised. "Rex, you have the out brief if the director calls it done this afternoon. See you back at the cabins later."

"Out here," Logan said.

"Out here," Rex echoed.

After checking that the crew was still setting up for the scene, Reid hopped onto the four-wheeler the Kualoa Ranch had assigned to him for the day. If he hurried, he could clear the area before the noise of his ATV interfered with the production.

Reid followed the trail leading back to the ranch's main building. After checking in the four-wheeler, he hurried out to his pride and joy, a Porsche 718 Boxster he'd bought used not long after arriving on Oahu. He ran his hand along the side of the sleek black sports car, still amazed he'd gotten it at such a good price. Yes, it was used, but barely. The old man he'd purchased it from was moving back to the mainland to live with his daughter in LA and didn't want to drive it in the city.

The other guys told him it was a mistake to buy a two-seater. What if he decided to settle down, get married and have kids?

Reid slipped into the driver's seat and pulled out of the parking lot.

He hadn't bothered to tell them he had no plans now or in the future of marrying and having kids.

Been there. Done that. Then, his wife left him for another man and took their baby daughter with her. He'd been deployed so much that the judge who had signed the divorce decree had given his ex-wife full custody, and because Reid didn't live close to her, he had such limited visitation he rarely got to see his daughter. She called his ex-wife's new husband Daddy and her biological father Reid because that was what her mother called him.

No. He'd never marry again, nor would he have any more children. He was careful to be sure of that with any woman he slept with, taking all the precautions to the point of pulling out before ejac-ulating, even with a condom.

Before he realized it, he was going eighty in a forty-mile-an-hour zone.

Reid lifted his foot off the accelerator, allowing the car to slow on its own. The little cabins he and his teammates rented were on the beach not far from the Kualoa Ranch. The cute blonde at the Burger Bar had told them about the vacancies when they'd stopped in for dinner after their first day on the movie set.

Reid hoped the friend Tish had sent had been able to find the key and let himself inside. It might be dumb to let a perfect stranger make himself at home in his cabin, but Reid figured that if Tish didn't trust him, she wouldn't tell him about the key under the mat. The guy would have to stay out on the porch until Reid got there.

And it wasn't like he kept anything of value in the cabin. It was a vacation rental, not a real home with a safe and security system. He hadn't had a real home since his wife had left him. Putting down roots, marriage and having kids set a guy up for a lot of pain when things didn't pan out.

He traveled light. The car was the biggest commitment he'd made since his divorce. He didn't look at it as a total commitment. It was an asset he would sell in a heartbeat. Maybe even make a little money on it, too.

As he pulled up next to the rental cabin, he studied the building. No one waited on the porch, which meant either the guy had found the key under the mat and let himself inside, or he'd spooked and split, not willing or able to wait for Reid to get there. Only one way to know. Check inside.

Reid parked the Porsche, got out and climbed the stairs of the front porch. When he tried the doorknob, it was locked. He checked under the mat for the spare key. It was gone.

The house was eerily silent. No sound of television, music or voices came from inside. He used his key to unlock the door and pushed it open, muscles tensed, ready to react to whatever or whoever he found on the other side.

Reid pushed the door open just enough to peer into the one-room cabin. The living room, bedroom and kitchen were all together. The only separate room was the bathroom with its walk-in shower, sink and toilet.

The only light in the room was from the open door, spilling across the floor in a wedge, leaving the corners in the shadows.

A figure moved near the small dinette table with its two vinyl-covered chairs.

Reid pushed the door open wider, allowing the light to reach the figure at the table.

A small woman with long dark hair stood beside the table, her chin held high and her fists clenched. She didn't say anything; she just stood there, her body tense, as if ready for a fight or flight. She was beautiful like the native Hawaiian women Reid had seen in photographs for sale in the souvenir shops.

"Are you Tish's friend?" Reid asked.

She nodded. "I am."

"I'm Reid Bennett."

He'd hoped by introducing himself, he could put this young woman at ease.

She remained where she was, with no visible release of the tension in her body.

"She texted me earlier saying a friend of hers

was headed my way, in need of protection." He lifted his chin toward her. "You want to tell me what's happened?"

Finally, she moved. She wrapped her arms around herself and looked toward the corner instead of at him. "I don't know. This is a mistake. I'm not sure I need protection. But I didn't know where else to turn. I can't go back to my apartment, and I can't even use my own car. I had to borrow Tish's."

"Perhaps you could start at the beginning. Have a seat. Would you like a drink? I'm sorry, I think all I have in the fridge is—"

"—beer," she finished for him. "No, thank you. I think I should go."

"Do you have a place to go?" he asked softly.

Her pretty brow puckered, and she shook her head.

"Is someone after you?"

"I don't know," she whispered. "Maybe."

He fought for patience. The fear in the woman's eyes was palpable. But she was holding back like she didn't want to tell him anything. Was she being abused? Was her husband or ex-boyfriend stalking her? He could only guess, and that would be a waste of time. "I can't help you unless you tell me what happened."

"I can't," she whispered, her pretty brown eyes filling with tears.

"Could you at least tell me your name?" he asked, frustrated by her refusal to talk to him. How could he protect her if he didn't know what he was protecting her from?

Despite his frustration at her reticence, his protective instinct was on high alert. He wanted to help her. He wanted to take the fear from her eyes and pound the shit out of whoever was tormenting her. He wanted to protect her.

Reid moved closer. "Talk to me. Tell me your name."

A movement behind her made Reid tense, ready to strike.

A tiny version of the pretty woman edged out of the shadows to stand beside the woman. "Her name is Maliea, and I'm Nani." She held up her hand with three fingers extended. "I'm three years old."

Seeing the child beside the woman hit Reid square in the gut. His first instinct was to back out of the cabin, jump into his Porsche and drive as fast and far away as he could get.

Three.

Holy fucking hell.

The little girl with long dark hair, like her mother's, was three. The same age as his daughter, Abby.

But there, the similarity ended.

Where Abby was blond-haired and blue-eyed, Nani had dark hair and big, innocent brown eyes.

She was Maliea's mini-me incarnate. Someday, that little girl would be as stunning as her mother and break men's hearts.

Men as gullible and trusting as he'd been.

"Are you okay?" Nani asked. "You look like you ate too much ice cream. When I eat too much ice cream, my tummy hurts. Does your tummy hurt?"

Oh, yes, his tummy hurt. It clenched from the gut-wrenching pain of losing his daughter when his wife had walked out.

He closed his eyes to block out the big, beautiful eyes of a child who was concerned about his tummy.

Reel it in, man. Reel it in.

He squared his shoulders, opened his eyes and gave the little girl a tight smile. "My tummy is okay. Thank you for asking." He turned to her mother.

"Ma'am," he said, keeping it formal. The less involved he got with mother and daughter, the better. "Perhaps we can go someplace to get a bite to eat."

Her brow furrowed, and she started shaking her head. "We worked hard to get me and Nani out of Tish's apartment so we wouldn't be followed."

"I got to ride in a beach bag," Nani announced with a grin. "I didn't move. Not even a little."

Maliea touched a hand to her daughter's hair. "You were so good."

"How did you get out undetected," Reid asked Maliea.

"Tish, Solange and I wore sunglasses and hats. Each of us carried a large beach bag and got into different cars. I took Tish's. She took mine."

Reid's lips quirked. "And Nani rode in one of the beach bags. Clever." He looked around the small cabin. "Do you still have the hat and sunglasses?"

She nodded. "I do."

"I have a ball cap Nani can wear. The Burger Bar has a playground off the back porch. It's not visible from the road, and we can wear our disguises. Nani can play while we talk," he said pointedly. "Where did you park Tish's car?"

Maliea chewed on her bottom lip. "Several doors down and behind a large trash bin."

He nodded. "Good. It will be okay there. We'll go in my car—" At that moment, he remembered. "Hmm. My car is a two-seater. If I promise to drive slowly, would you be okay with Nani sitting in your lap? When the other members of my team get back from the ranch, I can borrow one of their vehicles. One with more seats."

Maliea frowned. "I don't like Nani riding in the front seat and without a car seat for protection. But I guess if we go really slow... Are you sure we can't walk there?"

He tipped his head toward Nani. "It's too far for little legs, and I'd rather have wheels in case we need to go somewhere faster than on foot. We could stay here, but I don't have anything for Nani to eat or drink, and I'd really like to know what's got you spooked."

"How far is the burger place?" she asked.

"About a mile," he said.

She sighed. "I guess we could go. As long as we wear our disguises, and you go slow."

"Let me get that baseball cap," he said and ducked behind the bed where he'd stashed his duffel bag and pulled out his favorite San Diego Padres baseball cap. While he adjusted the back a little tighter, Maliea pulled Nani's long hair up into a ponytail and wrapped it around the elastic band several times into a bun.

Reid squatted in front of Nani and placed the cap on her head.

She grinned at him. "Can I keep it?"

Despite the grief for his daughter gnawing a hole in his belly, Reid couldn't help smiling at the little girl. "Yes, you can keep the hat."

When he straightened, Maliea had tucked her own wavy dark hair up into a wide-brimmed straw hat and fit sunglasses over her luminous brown eyes.

She was nothing like his ex-wife.

Laura had long, straight blond hair, blue eyes and was five-feet-nine.

Maliea probably wasn't even five feet five, and

her skin was a light, dusky brown, a testament to her Hawaiian heritage.

"Ready?" he asked, tearing his gaze away from the pretty mother and daughter.

Once he had an idea of what they were up against, he would contact his boss, Jace Hawkins, and ask who he wanted to assign to Maliea and Nani's protection duty.

Had it only been Maliea needing protection, Reid could have handled it. No problem.

Adding a three-year-old little girl into the mix?

He shook his head as he led them out to the fancy sports car that seemed entirely ridiculous now.

Maliea and Nani needed a bigger car and a protector with a lot less emotional baggage than he carried. Reid sure as hell wasn't the right man for this job.

Nothing could convince him otherwise. Not even two pairs of beautiful brown eyes, begging him for help.

CHAPTER 4

MALIEA STARED at the sleek black Porsche and frowned. "Are you sure you want us to get into that? Aren't you afraid we might damage something?"

He shook his head. "The leather seats are pretty tough. It'll be all right."

Maliea touched Nani's shoulder. "It will be easier if I get in first, baby," she said. "Then you can climb up onto my lap."

Maliea slipped into the leather passenger seat of the Porsche, afraid to touch anything. She'd never been in a car this fancy.

Once she was in, Nani scrambled into her lap.

Reid closed the door and rounded the front of the car to the driver's side.

As he bent to get into the driver's side, he glanced over at Maliea and Nani.

The little girl stared out the front windshield, and a smile spread across her little face. "Is this a race car?" she asked as Reid folded his long legs and body into the driver's seat and closed the door.

"I'm sorry to say it is not a race car," Reid said and started the engine. It roared to life and then settled into a rumbling purr like a lion's.

Reid eased onto the beach highway and maintained a slow pace all the way to a small, shack-like building with the words Burger Bar written in bold black letters over the door.

"It doesn't look like much, but the food is good," Reid said as he parked the Porsche next to a dilapidated older model compact car with a dent in the door and its back bumper missing entirely.

If the Porshe were hers, Maliea would have reconsidered driving it to Burger Bar and walked instead. Sweet Jesus, it was a beautiful car that must have cost this man a fortune.

When Nani reached out to touch one of the buttons, Maliea snatched her hand back. "Don't touch."

Reid chuckled. "Relax. I got the car used. I could never have afforded a new one."

"Still, it's too...too..." She shook her head, looking for the right word and failing miserably. "I'd be afraid to take it anywhere like it would be a magnet for trouble."

"That's what insurance is for." Reid got out of

the car and came around to help Nani out of Maliea's lap. He set her on her feet beside him. "Stay close," he warned. "Some cars drive fast down this road."

Nani's eyes widened. "Like a race car?"

Reid nodded. "Like a race car."

"I bet your car is faster," Nani said in her little voice, which sounded too grown up for a child so small.

Reid extended a hand to Maliea.

She ignored it, braced her hand on the door-frame and pulled herself halfway out of the car. Her hand slipped. She would have fallen back into her seat had Reid not darted forward as fast as he did.

He looped his arm around her waist and helped her the rest of the way out of the sports car and into his arms.

For a long moment, Maliea's hands rested against Reid's chest. She couldn't help but notice that the man was as solid and muscular as he looked in his black polo shirt, stretched tautly over bulging biceps.

Once Maliea had her feet firmly beneath her, she moved back, shocked at her immediate and visceral response to having this man's arms wrapped around her.

She blamed her rapid pulse on having nearly fallen backward, not on being held by a man who could melt a girl's panties with one look or one flex of those bulging biceps.

Had she just thought of bulging biceps twice already? Now, make that three times in as many seconds.

Heat filled her cheeks. She ducked her head, not wanting Reid to see how affected she was by having his hands and arms on her body.

He'd only saved her from falling backward. The embrace was nothing sexual or sensual. Just a way of helping her regain her balance. It didn't mean anything.

Hell, they didn't even know each other. She didn't know him. And she was a new widow, having just lost her husband not too long ago.

A husband who'd been growing increasingly distant over the past year, the devil on her shoulder reminded her.

Still, he'd been her husband.

For all she knew, Reid was married.

The thought made her cheeks burn even hotter.

She could be having lusty thoughts over a married man.

"So, Reid," she said, "how long have you and your wife been on Oahu?" She clapped her hand over her mouth as soon as the words left her lips. "You don't have to answer that. It's none of my business."

"I've been on Oahu for several weeks. No wife."

"Widower?" she asked, unable to stop herself.

"Divorced," he said flatly and held the door for her to enter the restaurant and bar.

"I'm sorry," she said softly as she brushed past him, her arm touching his chest and sending a spark of electricity zinging through her.

"Me, too," he said.

A cute blond woman smiled from behind the counter. "Hi, Reid. Have an early day at the ranch? Where's the rest of your gang?"

Reid nodded toward the young woman. "Hi, Jenny. Logan and Rex are still working. I'm playing hooky."

"Awesome," Jenny said with a grin. "Sit where you like. I'll bring menus."

Reid led Maliea and Nani to the outdoor patio where bistro tables sported umbrellas to shade the customers. Just off the south side of the patio was a playset with a swing and a play fort with ladders, rope bridges and a slide.

Nani's eyes grew wide, and she bounced up and down. "Can I play? Can I, please?"

Maliea laughed. "Of course, you can. Go on. But you'll have to come back to eat your lunch."

"I will," Nani said as she ran for the fort, climbing up the ladder to the top.

Maliea smiled at her daughter's happiness. "If only life were that simple and joyous."

Jenny appeared with the menus. "What can I get you to drink while you're looking over the menu?"

"I'll have water," Maliea said, mentally counting the little bit of money in her purse.

"Tap or bottled?" Jenny asked.

"Tap," Maliea responded.

"I'll have the same," Reid said.

As soon as Jenny left to get their drinks, Reid leaned closer. "Now that little ears are occupied, are you going to tell me what happened that made Tish send you to me for help?"

She told him about the break-in and destruction of her apartment and the man in the ski mask breaking into her car. While she talked, Maliea continued to watch Nani playing. Even without looking at the man, Maliea was no less aware of his presence.

As she finished her story, Jenny appeared with their drinks and took their orders. Maliea ordered a grilled cheese sandwich, sure it was all her budget could afford. She'd share it with Nani as her daughter would only ever eat half anyway.

"Aren't you ordering anything for you?" Reid asked.

"I'll share with Nani," she answered, feeling the heat rising in her cheeks all over again. She didn't like that she had to count every penny. Now that her apartment was trashed, she'd have to squeeze even more out of every dime. Replacing furniture was nowhere in the realm of her current finances. A blow-up mattress would have to do for both of them until things started looking up.

Reid ordered two hamburgers and two orders of fries.

Maliea raised her eyebrows. "Hungry?"

He nodded. "I am. We were up too early for breakfast."

Reid's gaze followed Nani as she climbed the ladder to the top of the fort and slid down the slide for the third time. "How much is Nani aware of what's happened?"

Maliea's heart pinched in her chest. "I haven't taken her home to the apartment. I don't want her to see it the way it is. It was traumatizing to me; I can't imagine how it would affect her."

Reid's lips pressed together. "Other than the guy grabbing your ankle in the parking lot, have there been any other physical attacks on you or Nani?"

Maliea sighed. "No. That's why I was hesitant to come to you. Tish thinks I'm the target. It's been my home and my car, but not so much me or Nani."

"It's as if whoever ransacked your apartment and then tried to break into your car might be looking for something. Something only *you* might have."

Maliea met Reid's gaze. "Other than my daughter, I have nothing of value except the diamond necklace my mother left me. But he didn't take it. What else would he be looking for?"

Reid's eyes narrowed. "Where was your husband when the apartment was tossed?"

Maliea's lips twisted. "Not in the picture."

"As in divorced?"

"As in dead," she stated flatly, surprised again at how emotionless she felt about Taylor's passing.

"I'm sorry," Reid said softly. "How is Nani dealing with the loss?"

"My husband wasn't around much over the past year. He spent more and more time at work and less at home. When I told her he wasn't coming home, she said it was sad and then asked me if I was going away." Maliea shook her head. "I told her I would be around for a very long time. She seemed okay." Maliea shrugged. "I guess time will tell. I think she misses her grandfather more. He spent more time with her than my husband." A lump lodged in Maliea's throat. "We lost my father in the same plane crash that took my husband."

"Wow," Reid said, "that's rough."

"It's been difficult, but we were managing until this. Now, I can't take her home. I don't want to stay with Tish and Solange, especially if someone is actually targeting me. I'm at a loss. I have a couple days off work to tackle clearing my husband and father's offices where they worked at the University, but I'm afraid that whoever is behind the break-ins might come after me or worse...Nani."

"Can you let the staff at the university go through your husband and father's offices for you?"

"I could, but they might not know what belonged to my father and husband and what belongs to the university. I'd like to at least look through what they've already done."

"You planned to do that today?" Reid asked.

"Or tomorrow," Maliea said. "I can't be off work for long. We didn't have much in savings, and my husband didn't have a life insurance policy." She gave a short mirthless laugh. "I still have to pay the rent for an apartment I can't live in. Not in its current state."

"You and Nani can't move back in until you figure out what the intruder was after."

"I told you. I don't own anything of value. There's nothing to steal." Maliea pinched the bridge of her nose. "I don't understand."

"What about your husband? Did he have something someone would want?"

"Not that I know of. Definitely not in our apartment."

"What did he do at the university?" Reid asked.

"He was an associate professor who taught World, US and Hawaiian history. My father was the head of the department." She shook her head.

"They were on a plane to the small island of Niihau, the Forbidden Island."

Reid nodded. "I'm familiar with the island. We did Navy SEAL training there. Isn't it difficult for just anyone to get permission to visit Niihau?"

Maliea nodded. "Yes. My father campaigned for months to attain permission to go to the island with his assistant."

"Your husband?" Reid prompted.

"Yes. They've been researching a pirate legend that supposedly happened in 1884. It was reported in a California newspaper, but there was very little documentation here in Hawaii. My father researched the legend for a number of years, making very little progress, mostly listening to tales passed down through families whose ancestors lived through the supposed attack on Honolulu by a red-bearded pirate. The story tells of how he stole hundreds of thousands of dollars in gold and silver from the palace and safes of local businessmen."

"Interesting." Reid tapped a finger on the table, his eyes narrowing. "Was there a treasure map involved?"

Maliea sighed. "I don't know about a map, but my father made notes from the interviews with each descendant's family. They all talked about the pirate ship sailing away toward Kauai. A year or so back, my father visited families in Kauai, asking about stories their elders passed down to them. Some swore they saw the ship pass their island about the time a storm blew in. The ship was swept toward Niihau on massive swells amid torrential rains."

"Did they find a shipwreck?"

"No," Maliea said. "Some think the ship wrecked on the coast of Niihau. The legend goes further to tell of the pirates transferring their booty to shore before another storm followed the first and swept the ship's remains out to sea. The ship was never seen again. Nor were the pirates. Or so they say."

"Maybe the inhabitants of Niihau ganged up on the pirates and either forced them to assimilate or be killed."

Maliea's lips pulled back in a tight smile. "As territorial as the inhabitants of Niihau are, I wouldn't put it past them. They fought hard against joining the United States as part of Hawaii, the fiftieth state. They like their solitude and intend to keep it that way."

Reid nodded. "I saw that. They were never happy to have us training on their island."

"Even before my father and then my husband became obsessed with the lost treasure of Red Beard, others tried to follow the path of the ship and the tales of its cargo being offloaded onto one of the islands."

"If there's no map, did your father keep a journal of his interviews and discoveries?"

"I need to go to his apartment and his office to sort through his papers and online files." Maliea pushed the hat back on her forehead and adjusted the sunglasses. "If he was chasing the treasure, he might have made notes from the information obtained from descendants." She met Reid's gaze. "Do you think the person who trashed my apartment and tried to get into my car was looking for my father's work?"

Reid shrugged. "It's possible. Treasure hunters can resort to some crazy stunts and murder to get their hands on a treasure."

"From what I know and my conversations with my father, he hadn't found it."

"Yet?"

She nodded. "Yet. He was certain he was getting closer to the clue he needed to finally locate the treasure. Thus, the trip to Niihau." Maliea looked away. "What my father and my husband didn't understand was that all the treasure they needed was right here on Oahu all along."

"You and Nani," Reid concluded. He reached across the table and took her hands in his. "Family is everything. Money doesn't warm your heart like watching your little girl grow up, learning new and exciting things every day." Reid's jaw hardened, and his lips pressed into a tight line.

"You sound like you speak from experience," Maliea said softly.

He nodded. "I do, but that's not what's important. I'd bet my right arm that whoever broke into your apartment and car is looking for your father's notes. Basically, the treasure map."

Maliea tilted her head to the side. "It makes more sense when I think of it that way."

"If he's still looking for it..." Reid grinned.

"He hasn't found it." Maliea's eyes widened. "I need to get to my father's office and sort through his journals and online files."

"And since your husband was working with your father to find the treasure, you'll want to go through his office as well."

Maliea gave a brief dip of her head. "I'll call and make an appointment with the department chair to clean out my father's and Taylor's offices as soon as possible."

She might not have a home to go to anytime soon, but at least she could help find the treasure. And if she found it, would they let her keep some of it? It would help solve her financial difficulties and maybe even fund her return to college, where she could earn a degree in a career field people were eager to hire, like nursing.

Maliea pulled her cell phone from her pocket and selected the number for the university operator when a woman's voice answered, "University of Hawaii. How can I direct your call?"

"I'd like to speak to the head of the history department, please," Maliea said. How many times had she used those same words, calling her father over the years?

The same lump formed in her throat that came about every time she thought of her father and the realization she'd never hear his voice again.

"This is Andrea Peterson, executive secretary of the Department of History. How may I help you?"

"Oh, Andrea, it's Maliea." Maliea's voice cracked. She had to swallow hard past the lump in her throat.

"Maliea, honey, I'm so glad you called. I've been worried about you. How are you and Nani holding up?"

"I'm doing okay," she lied. "Nani's fine. I need to come to the department and pick up my father's and Taylor's things."

"Of course," Andrea said in her sweetest motherly voice.

Maliea had known Andrea for over fifteen years. She'd been the woman she'd leaned on after her mother had passed. Her father had done the best he could, but his heart was more into history and research and less into fashion and things that might interest a teenage daughter. He'd sent her to Andrea when she'd had female questions. Andrea had been more than willing to help Maliea, having raised three daughters of her own.

"I'm sorry I haven't dealt with this sooner. It's just..." Maliea fought for the right word and settled on, "hard."

"I know. I miss them, too. Your father was always so good to me and fair with all his staff. He left a hole in our lives that will be hard to fill. And Professor Kaleiopu brought an energy and passion to the faculty that is noticeably missing." The older woman sighed. "How soon do you want to come?"

"The sooner, the better," Maliea said. "I might as well get it over with."

"How's this afternoon? If that's too soon, tomorrow morning would work as well. I'm taking off tomorrow afternoon for some appointments I can't reschedule."

"This afternoon would be good. Is an hour and a half from now too soon?" She'd need at least some of that time to get back to the other side of the island. "And I might have Nani with me. Will it be okay to bring her?"

"Yes, that would be wonderful," Andrea said. "I still have a drawer full of coloring books and crayons I keep just for her visits. We can load her up with those to take home with her."

"That would be lovely," Maliea said. "She talks about her Granny Annie all the time and asks when she can visit."

"That little sweetheart can visit any time. She gives the best hugs."

"Then I'll see you in an hour and a half," Maliea said.

"Yes, ma'am," Andrea said. "See you then."

Maliea ended the call and looked up to find Reid studying her.

"We're going to the university?" he asked.

She gave a little shrug. "Nani and I are," she said. "You don't have to. I'm sure we'll be all right. Like you said, the attacks have been on the apartment and my car more so than on me or Nani."

"And if you find anything in your father's or husband's office, the attacks might shift to you." Reid's brow furrowed. "Even if you don't find anything, the attacks might shift to you and Nani. Whoever was behind the previous incidents might think you found something and go after you either way."

Her gaze on her daughter happily swinging on the playset, Maliea chewed on her bottom lip. "I can't leave Nani with Tish or Solange. It would set them up as targets as well. Besides, I hate to let Nani out of my sight. What if he kidnaps her and uses her as a bargaining chip to extort whatever he thinks I have—which I don't—in exchange for my daughter?" She threw her arms in the air, over-whelmed by all the horrible scenarios running rampant in her head. "Hell, if I had what he's looking for, I'd give it to him just to get him off my back and keep Nani safe."

Reid reached for Maliea's hand and held it firmly in his. "It's okay. Either one of my team members or I will go with you two and keep you safe. Maybe once you find whatever it is he's looking for, it will help us figure out who's bothering you, and you can put it all behind you."

"Sooner than later, I hope," Maliea muttered. "I've had enough drama in the past few weeks to last a lifetime." Her heartbeat fluttered as if it couldn't quite find its normal rhythm while Reid Bennett held her hand. What was wrong with her? She was newly widowed and yet lusting after a stranger. Had she no shame? No sense of grief for the man she'd promised to love, honor and cherish?

Guilt gnawed at her gut.

Maliea pulled her hand free of Reid's and laid it safely in her lap. It was too soon after losing Taylor.

Never mind they hadn't had sex in months. Maliea blamed it on their opposing schedules, but it was more than that. He hadn't bothered to touch her, hold her or even kiss her, coming and going.

If she was completely honest with herself, she'd lost Taylor even before he'd died in that plane crash.

Still, it was too soon after losing her husband. Now was not the time to have feelings for someone else. To desire another man's touch.

CHAPTER 5

JENNY, the cute, blond waitress, arrived carrying a tray loaded with Reid's two hamburger platters, overflowing with steaming hot fries, and the grilled cheese sandwich with potato chips and a pickle spear. While she set them on the table, Maliea stepped over to the playset to bring Nani in to eat her lunch and to get a grip on her overstimulated libido.

Nani came as soon as her name was called.

Maliea's heart brimmed with pride at how well-behaved her daughter was. For a three-year-old, she acted more like an old soul than a small child all too often.

If her marriage had been more stable, her husband home more often, and if they'd had any kind of sex life, Maliea would have wanted more children.

Nani needed siblings. Maliea had always wished she'd had a brother or sister to share her childhood with. She'd always dreamed of having three or four children. A house full of love and laughter. Her own mother had wanted that many but had to settle on her one daughter when cervical cancer struck her shortly after Maliea's birth. A hysterectomy had ended her ability to have more children at an early age.

When Maliea returned to the table, she noted that Jenny had set one of the two hamburger platters in front of Maliea's chair. Her mouth watered at the juicy burger with the mound of fries. She helped Nani into her chair and cut the grilled cheese in half before turning to the plate before her.

"This is yours," she said, pushing the delicious-smelling burger toward Reid.

"I'm not quite as hungry as I thought I was when I ordered. I hate to see it go to waste. You do like hamburgers and fries, don't you?"

"Yes, but these are yours," she insisted. "Nani and I will split the grilled cheese sandwich."

"I'm hungry, Mama," her daughter said. "Can I eat all of it?" she asked, already nearly done with half of the gooey, cheesy sandwich.

"My treat," Reid said. "You'll save me from insulting the chef by eating all that. He has a reputation for making the best burgers on the island—hell, on any of the Hawaiian Islands."

"I'll pay for our food," Maliea said.

"Too late. I already did," Reid said and took a big bite out of his hamburger.

Maliea's stomach rumbled loudly. She was so hungry her hands shook in her lap. She'd fed Nani the last of her granola bars and splurged on chocolate milk for her at a convenience store on the drive over from Honolulu. It had satisfied Nani, but there hadn't been anything left for Maliea.

And, wow, the fries smelled so good.

"I'll pay you back." Maliea lifted the burger in both hands and sank her teeth into the bun and thick beef patty, juice dripping down her chin.

Before she could stop herself, she moaned.

"Right?" Reid laughed. "The best hamburgers ever."

"Yes," she said around the big bite of food in her mouth. Then she remembered her manners and chewed thoroughly before swallowing. She didn't talk again until she'd consumed three-quarters of the massive burger. She laid it on the plate and drank from her water glass.

Reid chuckled. "Were you hungry?"

Heat rose up her neck into her cheeks. "I guess."

Nani picked at the potato chips on her plate, having eaten more than half of her sandwich.

"Are you finished?" Maliea asked.

Nani nodded and yawned. "Can I go play now?"

Even tired, Nani didn't want to miss an opportunity to play on a really cool play set. The one at their apartment complex wasn't nearly as interesting. Also, her apartment didn't have the view Burger Bar afforded from its location on the beach.

"You can play for a few more minutes," Maliea said. "Then we have to leave."

"Do we have to?" Nani stared up at Maliea, disappointment turning her usual happy smile upside down.

"Yes, ma'am." Maliea waved her hand at her daughter. "Now go, or you won't get to play at all."

Nani skipped off the patio out onto the sandy playground.

Maliea's gaze followed her daughter. Once Nani was busy swinging, Maliea turned to Reid.

His gaze was on Nani, his lips pressed into a tight line. A shadow seemed to have fallen over him.

"Do you like children?" Maliea asked.

Reid's gaze shifted to the empty plate in front of him. He pushed it to the side before he answered, "Yeah, sure."

She sensed more to his answer than the two words. "Do you have children from your marriage?"

For a long moment, he said nothing.

The way he shut down made her regret asking the question. Apparently, it hit a cord with him.

She was about to tell him not to answer the question when he spoke.

"I have a daughter."

"Oh, yeah?" Maliea brightened. She couldn't picture this man with the brooding face being the father of a child. But then, she didn't know him well enough to pass judgment. Despite his clipped responses, Maliea was dauntless in her desire to know this man better. If he was to provide their protection, she should know a little more about him. "How old is your daughter?"

"Three." His gaze returned to Nani who'd abandoned the swing to climb the ladder to the top of the play fort.

The pain in that one-word response hit Maliea square in the chest.

"Does she live with you?" Maliea asked, already knowing the answer.

"No."

She touched his arm. "I'm sorry."

He pushed back from the table. "Are you ready to go?"

If she wasn't, it was too damned bad. He was.

"I am." Maliea pushed away from the table, stood and called out, "Nani, it's time to leave."

Nani waved from the top of the fort, slipped

down the slide and ran toward Maliea and Reid. As she always did, she slid her hand into Maliea's.

To Maliea's surprise, Nani placed her other hand in Reid's.

His eyes flared, and he shot a glance down at Nani.

Nani smiled up at him. "Thank you for bringing me here to play."

He looked at the tiny hand in his, cleared his throat and said, "You're welcome."

Maliea held her breath, fully expecting Reid to extract Nani's hand from his.

It would confuse Nani, but she'd get over it as long as Maliea didn't abandon her.

To Maliea's surprise, Reid didn't shake Nani off.

The three of them walked back through Burger Bar hand-in-hand.

They looked like a happy little family.

Well, minus Reid. His face appeared carved in granite, except for the little tic in his jaw. Since she'd brought up the topic of his little girl, he'd retreated into a stony silence.

At the Porsche, he held the door open for Maliea.

She sank into the soft leather seat and waited for Nani to climb into her lap.

Nani turned to Reid and held up her arms.

Reid frowned, hesitated and then swung her up into his arms.

Maliea's daughter wrapped her arms around his neck and planted a loud kiss on his cheek. She leaned back and said in her most grown-up voice, "There. You can put me down now."

Reid lowered her into Maliea's lap, his hand brushing lightly against Maliea's breast as he released his hold on her daughter.

That accidental connection shot sparks throughout Maliea's body, making her suck in a sharp breath.

Reid backed away quickly as if he'd been scalded, hurried around the hood of the sports car and climbed in. Was he embarrassed, or had he felt the same bolt of electricity?

Girl, get a grip, she mentally admonished herself. *He's only here to protect you and Nani, not to seduce you into his bed.*

That thought, once mentally voiced, was impossible to erase.

Maliea closed her eyes and held onto her daughter to keep from staring at the gorgeous ex-SEAL.

Nani was Maliea's reason for living.

Unfortunately, Reid had awakened in her needs she hadn't realized she'd missed.

AFTER HIS BOOB-BRUSH WITH MALIEA, Reid couldn't think of anything else but how soft and full her breasts were. She might be petite, but the woman had full, luscious tits and a nice swell to her hips and ass.

Whoa, dude.

Those weren't thoughts he should be having about a potential client.

Without another word, he drove the very short distance back to the row of cabins. He parked in front of his unit, got out and came around to help Nani and Maliea to their feet.

At that moment, Logan and Rex pulled up in Logan's black four-wheel-drive SUV.

Logan had barely shifted into park and turned off the engine when he jumped out of the driver's seat. "Reid, I thought you said Tish's friend was a guy." He grinned and held out his hand to Maliea. "Logan Atkins, at your service."

"Maliea Kaleiopu," Maliea said, her brow wrinkling.

Reid had a sudden desire to knock Logan's hand away. To keep from doing just that, he shoved his hands into his pockets and gritted his teeth as Logan lifted Maliea's hand and pressed a kiss to her pretty knuckles.

His gut clenching, Reid ground down hard on his back teeth. He wanted to tell Logan to back off, that Maliea was his.

But she wasn't. She didn't belong to anyone and could choose any man, including his buddy Logan.

Then why did seeing Logan kiss her knuckles make Reid want to plow a fist into his friend's face?

A little hand touched his arm.

Dragging his gaze away from Logan and Maliea, Reid glanced down into the large, soft brown eyes of Maliea's mini-me, Nani.

The little girl raised her arms.

Reid automatically bent and lifted her.

Nani looped one of her skinny arms around his neck. She leaned close to his ear and whispered, "Who are those men?"

Though he didn't feel at all happy or serene, he smiled at Nani. "These two men work with me. They're my friends." At least Logan used to be his friend. If he didn't let go of Maliea's hand in the next ten seconds, Reid would end that friendship with a right uppercut to the other man's jaw.

Maliea pulled her hand free of Logan's and shoved it in her pocket. "Nice to meet you, Logan. Do you work with Reid?"

"When we're assigned to the same security detail or a team mission. Reid said you're experiencing some trouble. How can I help?"

"By loaning me your SUV," Reid answered.

"Not a problem," Logan said. "I can take you anywhere you need to go." His comment was aimed at Maliea, not Reid.

"We need the SUV," Reid said through gritted teeth. "Not a driver." He pulled the keys to his

Porsche from his pocket and tossed them toward Logan.

The younger man snagged the keys in the air and grinned. "Awesome." He glanced at Rex. "Feel like going for a drive with the top down?"

"I could be convinced," Rex said. "As long as it gets us to food."

"Burger Bar?" Logan asked.

Rex snorted. "Since it's the closest restaurant and my belly is grumbling, it will have to do."

"I thought you liked the food there," Logan said.

"I do," Rex said. "But I can only eat so many burgers before I'm sick to death of them."

"Burgers are like the holy grail of junk food. I could eat one at every meal," Logan admitted. "And Burger Bar makes the absolute best." He flashed a blinding smile at Maliea.

"And you have the emotional and culinary maturity of a ten-year-old," Rex said. "Burger Bar is fine by me. But if we're ever going to get there, you'll need to quit flirting, shower, change and get back out here in under five minutes, or I'm leaving without you."

"You can't without the keys." Logan dangled the set of keys in Rex's face.

Rex's hand shot out. He snatched the keys from Logan's grip and grinned.

"Well, damn," Logan said.

"Damn right, damn," Rex turned to Maliea and

held out his hand. "Rex Johnson. Pleasure to meet you." He glanced at Reid. "Need help with the new assignment? Do you want Logan or me to handle Ms. Maliea and her daughter's protection detail?"

Reid had had all intentions of handing off the mother and daughter pair to someone else.

Nani leaned close to his ear and whispered, "I don't want those men. I want you."

Reid's heart swelled inside his chest. He didn't want her words to mean so much to him, but they did. Nani trusted him to be there for her and her mother.

He just had to remember it was a short-term assignment until they found the man responsible for the attacks.

After that, Reid would walk away and never look back.

Only it wasn't that simple. How could he walk away from a little girl who gave the best hugs and, when she held his hand, made him feel special and alive again?

And what was that jolt of electricity he'd felt when his hand had brushed against Maliea's breast? His thoughts had gone straight to touching her naked breasts, not her fully clothed ones.

His groin tightened.

If he really wanted to turn over Nani's and Maliea's protection to someone else, Logan and Rex would be his first choices. No, make that Rex.

He would be his first choice. Logan was too much of a player.

"Did the movie crew finish today?" Reid asked.

Rex shook his head. "One of the main cameras was acting up. They'll be back at it tomorrow morning."

Which meant they were still needed for that job.

"I'll get in touch with Hawk and let him know about the set and Ms. Kaleiopu. He might want to assign another man one way or the other."

Rex nodded. "Let us know."

"In the meantime, Logan," Reid gave the man a pointed look, "I need the keys to your SUV."

"Seems like a reasonable trade," Logan said with a grin. "I've wanted to see if your Porsche can really do zero to one hundred in a second."

Reid held out his hand. "Give me your keys."

Logan handed over the keys to this SUV. "A deal's a deal."

Reid's eyes narrowed. "There are speed limits for a reason. Especially around here. Don't do anything stupid."

Logan grinned. "Challenge accepted."

"I'm already regretting giving you my keys," Reid murmured and forced himself to turn away. He couldn't worry about a car when this woman and child were now his assignment until he solved their problems or Hawk assigned someone else to see to Maliea and Nani's needs. "Come on, ladies, we have an appointment to keep."

Once settled and buckled into Logan's SUV, Reid glanced to the backseat where Nani sat with a seatbelt across her little lap. She looked so small and fragile it made Reid's heart squeeze hard.

"We need to find a car seat for her," he said. "That seatbelt will do little to protect her if we should be involved in an accident."

"We had to leave her car seat in my vehicle to get her out of the apartment complex without being detected." Maliea glanced back at her daughter. "Maybe we could meet up with Tish and get that car seat or have her drop it off somewhere we can find it."

"See what you can arrange," Reid said. "I need to inform my boss of our additional requirements."

Maliea gave a fleeting smile. "Me and Nani?"

He nodded and pulled out his cell phone, selecting the number at the top of his list.

The call didn't even ring on his end when Jace Hawkins answered, "Reid, you and the guys wrapping it up at Kualoa Ranch?"

"Not quite." Reid shifted into drive, checked both ways and pulled onto the highway. "Camera equipment glitches slowed them down today. If they get it fixed, they hope to finish up tomorrow."

"Good to know," Hawk said. "I had a request

come in from a man on Kauai. Fortunately, he's flexible and can wait a couple of days."

"Had a text from Tish Jenkins this morning," Reid said.

"The woman you guarded while she was in a coma?"

"Yes, sir," Reid answered. "She sent another client our way."

"Fill me in."

While Maliea texted Tish about the car seat, Reid laid out the situation for Hawk.

When Reid was finished, Hawk said, "I can send one of our guys from Maui to look out for Ms. Kalieopu's safety. In the meantime, I take it you're running interference for her?"

Reid's gaze went to Maliea's pretty face and the frown of concentration denting her brow. "Yes, sir."

"Two men on Kualoa Ranch duty is enough?" Hawk queried.

"It's pretty quiet," Reid said. "One more day, and they'll be done, barring any technical glitches."

"Good to know. I'll get one of the guys on a plane this evening to take over with the woman and her child."

"Maliea and Nani," Reid said.

"Right." Hawk hesitated. "Kalea uses the legend of the pirate attack during the story-telling portion of the annual Luau here on Parkman Ranch. I thought it was all some mystical fabrication. It would be interesting if it turns out to be based in truth."

"Maliea's father chased clues for years. He thought he had the final pieces of the puzzle and was on his way to Niihau when his plane went down."

"Had he documented his findings and the information that led him to believe the stories?" Hawk asked.

"Maliea thinks so," Reid said. "She indicated that her father kept a journal of his detailed interviews with other island folk."

"Has she found the journal?" Hawk asked.

"Not that I know of." Reid stared down at Maliea's silky dark hair, wanting to sink his fingers into the soft lengths and pull her closer.

She tucked her phone into her pocket and looked at him, catching him staring down at her.

"I'll be with Ms. Kaleiopu through the evening. Let me know who you're sending. If you give him my number, we can arrange a meeting location and hand-off."

"Then you'll head back to Kualoa Ranch to conduct the out brief with the production company?" Hawk asked.

"Logan and Rex are fully capable of conducting the out brief. I can be available if they need more help."

Hawk chuckled. "Fair enough. Get some rest.

We'll be in contact tomorrow morning, bright and early."

As Reid ended the call, he thought about the "hand-off." His gaze went to Maliea in the seat beside him and then Nani smiling happily in the back. He couldn't picture meeting up with one of his team, handing over the reins and walking away from them. They'd come to him for help. If something happened to them after he'd stepped back from the case, could he live with himself?

Not that he didn't trust his teammates. Given his aversion to working with children because of his separation from his daughter, was he the right person to provide their protection?

Or was he the right person because he was a father and knew how devastating the loss of one's child was to a parent?

Could he walk away?

CHAPTER 6

"WHAT'S WRONG?" Maliea asked, her pretty brow forming a V over her nose.

Her question pulled Reid back to the present and away from a future he'd thought he'd wanted and was now unsure of.

"Nothing," he said, focusing on the road ahead. "Hawk's sending reinforcements."

Her continued frown indicated she was concerned.

Reid chose to change the subject rather than attempt to explain himself when he couldn't make sense of his feelings to begin with. "Did you get in touch with Tish about the car seat?"

Maliea nodded. "She's going to leave the car seat in a shopping cart at my favorite craft supply store in thirty minutes."

Maliea glanced up, meeting his gaze. "Is your

boss sending your replacement?" she asked, her voice low so as not to carry to her daughter in the back seat.

"He is. Whether he'll take my spot providing security for the film crew or take over your support, I don't know. For now, you're stuck with me."

"I'm glad," Maliea said. "There's been so much change and strange people and places. I worry that *someone* will be upset if things don't settle down soon."

Reid cast a glance over the console to the little girl sitting behind her mother. His heart pinched hard in his chest at the dent in her little forehead.

"Are we going home now?" Nani asked, her gaze shifting from the scenery out the window to Reid's face.

He quickly shifted his focus to the road in front of him and let her mother answer.

"Not yet, sweetie," Maliea said. "I have some errands to run first. You get to come with us."

"Okay," Nani said with a yawn. "But I miss my bear. Do you think he misses me?"

Maliea met Reid's glance briefly. "I'm sure he does, but we're going to see Granny Annie. She misses you even more. And she has coloring books for you."

"Yay," Nani said and yawned again. "Will we be there soon?"

"Yes, we will," Maliea said. "Close your eyes for a few minutes, and we'll be there."

"Okay, mama," Nani said from the back seat. "Wake me when we're there."

"I will, baby," Maliea said softly.

In the rearview mirror, Reid could see Nani close her eyes and lean her head back against the seat. Soon, her head tipped sideways, and then her body slumped over. The child was asleep.

Warmth spread through Reid's chest. He wished he could find a car seat so Nani wouldn't have to slump over or be in danger should they have an accident. He'd work on that right after their visit to the university.

"What is your little girl like?" Maliea asked quietly. When he didn't respond immediately, she added, "You don't have to tell me if you don't want to."

Reid stared at the road ahead, his thoughts going back to his last visit with Abby. He'd gone to California for the two weeks he was supposed to have with his daughter.

"She has blond hair and blue eyes," he said.

"Well, she obviously didn't get the blond hair from you," Maliea said with a smile. "But the blue eyes..." She leaned forward in her seat.

"Are mine," he said. "My ex has blond hair and hazel eyes. Abby's are baby blue."

"Abby." Maliea smiled. "She sounds amazing."

'She is." Reid's glance went to the rearview mirror. "Smart and so curious. Like Nani."

"You must miss her," Maliea whispered.

He gave a brief nod, his jaw tightening.

"Does it bother you to be around other children?" she asked. "Is being around Nani reminding you too much of what you're missing?"

"My feelings are not important," he said. "What matters is that I'm here to protect you and Nani. That's all you need to worry about."

His words effectively shut her down.

Maliea didn't ask any more questions or make any comments until they arrived at the University of Hawaii, where her father and husband had worked up to the day they'd died.

She quietly directed him to the building they needed to enter.

He cast a glance in her direction, wondering what was going through her mind as he pulled into a parking space and turned off the engine. "Are you going to be okay?"

Her gaze fixed on the building. Her face was set in strained lines, and her lips pressed together as if to keep them from trembling.

If Reid wasn't mistaken, her eyes were glassy as if holding back unshed tears.

"Is this the first time you've been back here since...?" he asked.

She gave him a brief nod, squared her shoulders

and said, "Let's get this over with." Maliea turned away and pushed open her door.

Reid hurried out of the vehicle and around to the passenger side, where Maliea was opening the door for Nani.

Nani bounced out of the back seat, seemingly unaware of the effect the visit was having on her mother. She slipped her hand into Maliea's and held out her other hand for Reid.

Girding his loins, he took the proffered hand and walked on the other side of Nani toward the building, his gaze sweeping the area, searching for any hint of danger.

Young people, carrying satchels filled with books or sporting backpacks slung over one shoulder, hurried along the sidewalks or across the green lawns to different buildings in a hurry to get from one class to the next. Though busy, nothing indicated any threat to Maliea or her daughter. Still, Reid wouldn't let down his guard. Since the previous attacks had occurred at night, he doubted whoever was targeting them would make another attempt during daylight hours. And this wasn't Afghanistan or another third-world country where enemy operatives could be around every corner. Hawaii was supposedly civilized.

All the more reason to be on alert at all times.

Reid's grip tightened gently on Nani's hand, and his gaze swept over Maliea as they approached the building. He'd protect them at all costs, including his own life.

MALIEA DREW in a deep breath and told herself not to cry. The last thing she wanted to do was upset Nani. Her daughter might only be three, but she was old beyond her years and sensitive to others around her, especially her mother.

Reid released his hold on Nani's hand, pushed open the door and stood back as she and Nani entered.

Maliea led the way down the hallway to the staircase leading up to the offices where her father and Taylor had worked.

She headed for her father's office to check in with Andrea Peterson, her friend and the History Department's secretary.

Andrea stood and threw open her arms as soon as Maliea and Nani stepped through the door. "There's my Nani-Nani-Boo-Boo," she cried and engulfed Nani in a bear hug, lifting the child off the ground. "I'm so happy to see my little sugar britches." She gave Nani a loud, smacking kiss.

Nani hugged the woman around the neck and smiled. "Granny Annie, what do you have for me in your magic drawer?"

Andrea set Nani on her feet and waved her

hand toward her desk. "I don't know. It's magic. You'll have to see for yourself."

Nani squealed with delight and yanked open the drawer. While Nani dug into the crayons and coloring books, Andrea met Maliea's gaze, her eyes welling. Wordlessly, she opened her arms.

Maliea fell into her motherly embrace, fighting the tears. A few leaked out, but she quickly brushed them away. With Andrea holding her like this, memories flowed through of the last time she'd held her in her arms when her mother had died.

"I'm so sorry," Andrea whispered.

"Me, too," Maliea responded. Then she pushed back, quickly brushed away the few tears she hadn't been able to hold back and lifted her chin. "I need to get this done. Not only so that I can move on but so the department can as well."

Andrea frowned. "Don't you worry about the department. You take all the time you need."

Maliea swallowed hard on the lump lodged in her throat. "Thank you."

"Heather, the TA who's been working with Taylor for the past year, has been sorting and boxing things in his office, but feel free to see if she missed any personal effects or packed anything you don't want to keep. She's been helping me go through your father's things as well. We have a box of his things ready for you to go through at your own pace."

Maliea nodded. "Thank you."

Andrea's gaze went to Reid. "I don't think we've met."

Heat filled Maliea's cheeks. "I'm sorry. Andrea Peterson, this is Reid, my...friend."

Reid didn't blink at Maliea's classification. He held out a hand and gave a brief smile. "Ms. Peterson, it's a pleasure to meet you."

The older woman took his hand, her cheeks turning a rosy pink. "Oh, the pleasure is mine," she said. "I'm glad Maliea has a friend with her. Especially after losing her father and husband."

Maliea glanced toward Nani.

"Don't worry about my Nani-Boo-Boo," Andrea said with a smile aimed at the three-year-old. "I'll keep an eye on her."

Maliea bit on her bottom lip, not wanting to say so much that her daughter picked up on her concerns but needing Andrea to know what had happened in the past twenty-four hours. She tipped her head toward the office door.

Andrea nodded and followed her out into the hallway.

Reid stood in the doorway, his attention split between the ladies and Nani.

As soon as they were out of earshot of Nani, Andrea asked, "What's wrong?"

Maliea quickly filled her in on the break-in at

her apartment and her car while parked outside Tish's apartment.

Andrea's eyes widened. "Why would someone break into your place and car?"

Maliea shrugged. "All we can figure is that they might be looking for something to do with the treasure my father and Taylor were researching. Maybe a map or my father's notes. Did he have a journal he might have kept with his notes from the interviews he conducted in his research? Or maybe an online file where he kept his notes?"

Andrea's lips twisted. "Heather and I went through everything on your father's desk and shelves. We didn't find a journal, notebook or anything like that."

Maliea cocked a hopeful eyebrow. "Online?"

Andrea shook her head. "I've been through his files on his desktop computer and haven't found anything like that, or anything personal. He was careful to set a good example for all members of the department. He used his department computer for department use only. He didn't even put family birthdays or anniversaries on his work calendar. He had a laptop he carried in his briefcase that he used on his lunch break."

"If he didn't make notes or show his research, how was he able to get department funding for the flight to Niihau?" Maliea asked.

"That's just it," Andrea said. "He didn't ask for department funding. He paid for the flight himself. He said he didn't want to waste the university's money on what might prove to be a wild goose chase."

Maliea frowned. "What about the other interviews on the different islands?"

Andrea nodded. "All out of his own pocket. No money from the department. He loved his job here and didn't want to risk it chasing a story that could prove to be only folklore."

"Why didn't he tell me all this?" Maliea whispered, feeling a bit betrayed. She hadn't known her father nearly as well as she should have.

Andrea sighed. "He considered it a hobby, not an obsession. And he learned things about the islands and the inhabitants along the way he could use in his classes on Hawaiian history."

Maliea glanced at the door where Reid stood. "I think he used some of that research in the bedtime stories he told Nani when he pulled Grandpa duty the nights I had to work a gig." Her lips curled upward on the corners. "When I'd get home earlier than expected, I'd find him reading from the book he'd made for her. He'd filled it with tales of the islands and hand-drawn pictures of turtles and volcanoes. She loves those stories."

Her gaze met Reid's. "Are you staying here? I'll only be in Taylor's office for a few minutes, especially if they've already boxed his personal effects."

Reid frowned. "Where is his office?"

Maliea tipped her head to a door down the hall. "Not far."

He nodded. "I'll stay here and keep watch in both directions."

Maliea walked down the hallway to Taylor's office. She hadn't actually been in his office in months, even though it had been down the hallway from her father's. He'd always been in a class or out to lunch with colleagues when she'd stopped in.

Out of habit, she raised her hand to knock and stopped short of tapping her knuckles against the door. Why knock? Her husband was dead. He wouldn't be in his office talking with a student or working on a syllabus.

She turned the knob and pushed the door open.

A woman with long blond hair glanced up, her eyes rounding. When she saw Maliea, she pressed a hand to her chest and forced a laugh. "Oh, Ms. Kalieopu, you startled me." She waved toward the boxes lined up near the door. "Be careful, and don't trip on the boxes. I was just loading the last one for you. Andrea said you might stop by today." Her brow furrowed. "I didn't get the chance at the funerals to tell you how sorry I was about your father and Taylor's—" she caught herself, "Professor Kalieopu's accident. I was shocked at the news, and the department was devasted. I can't imagine how you're feeling."

"Not great," Maliea admitted briefly. She didn't want to go into her feelings with the TA. "Is there any order I should follow going through the boxes?"

"You can start with the ones by the door," the younger woman said. "I think I got all his personal belongings, but I wanted to make one last pass. The books are those he purchased out of pocket. I've set aside the textbooks used in the classrooms."

Maliea opened the box closest to her and dug through the contents—a small box filled with business cards, a couple of framed photos of Nani that Maliea had given him for his office and stacks of history books. She thumbed through the books, searching for any handwritten notes and found none.

Other than the photographs of Nani, she had no use for the books. She plucked the photos out of the box and laid them on a table beside the stack. "If the department wants these books, they can have them. I don't need them or have space to store them."

"I'll let them know," Heather said.

She moved the box aside and opened the next one. It too had a stack of books on self-help, management and techniques for teaching. She thumbed through each and found nothing of interest. Again, she had no use for the books. She might have saved them for Nani, but she didn't have the space or want to haul books around when she moved from the apartment she couldn't go back to since the break-in to a new apartment.

"Same goes for this box of books," Maliea said. "The university is welcome to them."

"I'll put a note on both of them." Heather pulled a pen out of the desk, along with a pad of sticky notes and crossed to where Maliea stood.

"The only other boxes are the ones on and behind his desk. You might want to go through them," Heather said. "They contain more personal items that Taylor—Professor Kaleiopu—had lying around the office and some of the knickknacks he collected during his research trips. I was just finishing up with his desk drawers when you arrived."

Heather moved away from the back of his desk, allowing Maliea space to slip in.

Maliea eased past the pretty TA and opened the top of the box resting on the desk. She found Taylor's appointment calendar. She flipped it open and thumbed through, casually glancing at the words scribbled on the side about different students, lecture notes, and grocery items she might have asked him to get on his way home from work. She flipped through the pages until she came to the date of the plane crash.

Maliea had never understood why he'd used a paper planner instead of relying on the online work calendar. He'd argued that he did both, but the paper calendar gave him a place to doodle, as evidenced by the outline of a ship on the day he and Maliea's father were due to visit Niihau.

The day of the plane crash.

The day she'd lost her husband and her father.

The day she'd lost any type of financial stability for her and her daughter. As she closed the day planner, a slip of paper fell out and drifted to the floor.

Before Maliea could bend to pick up the piece of paper with something scrawled in handwriting across it, Heather snatched it from the floor, crumpled it and tossed it into the trash.

Curious, Maliea asked, "What was it?"

"Just a reminder to speak with one of his students," Heather said. "If you'd like me to carry some of these boxes out, I could do that for you."

Maliea picked through the box in front of her a little more, then put the lid back over the top. "You can take this one if you don't mind."

"Sure." Heather lifted the box and carried it out the door of Taylor's office.

After Heather left, Maliea pulled the crumpled paper out of the trash basket and unfolded it. The writing on the note wasn't her husband's scribble at all. It was a message that didn't make any sense.

Tonight

The one word was written in flowing script and

dotted with a heart. The handwriting was more feminine than Taylor's masculine scrawl. Her gaze rose to the door where Heather had passed through moments before.

Had her husband had an affair with his TA?

A backpack leaned against a bookshelf near one of the boxes on the floor. Maliea didn't recognize it as one of Taylor's. She could hear the sound of voices murmuring down the hallway from Andrea's office. With guilt gnawing in her belly, she tipped the backpack over and unzipped the top. Inside were spiral notebooks and a leather-bound journal.

Could it be Taylor's journal? Perhaps it contained notes about the treasure. Maliea paused, her hand resting on the leather.

If it was Taylor's journal, why would Heather take it? Had she hoped to continue his research?

Before the TA returned, Leah quickly slid the journal from the backpack and flipped it open. Inside, the handwriting was feminine. Not Taylor's. Some of the words captured Maliea's attention. Words like *shipwreck*, *local legend* and *treasure* jumped out of the page. Apparently, Heather had been working with Taylor on his research, searching for the lost treasure of Red Beard.

The voices grew louder in the hallway. She could make out Andrea and Heather's higher-pitched tones. The deep richness of Reid's voice was unmistakable, sending a bolt of awareness across her senses.

Footsteps sounded on the wooden floors, moving in her direction.

As Maliea closed the journal, she spied a word where an "i" had been dotted with a heart.

Maliea shoved the journal into the backpack and quickly zipped it, leaning it back against the bookshelf just as she'd found it. She lifted the lid off the box beside it and sifted through knickknacks and the fancy bookends she'd given Taylor last Christmas.

"Maliea?" Heather's voice sounded from the doorway.

Maliea popped her head up over the top of the desk. "I'm here. Just going through the last box."

She replaced the lid on the box and stood, bringing the box with her. She placed it on top of the desk and gave the younger woman a tight smile. "This must be hard on the whole department, including you."

Heather stared around the office, her brow puckered. "They will be missed. It all happened so quickly. Your father was such a cornerstone of the department, and Taylor... So young." She met Maliea's gaze. "But you..." She shook her head. "I'm sorry for your loss."

Maliea acknowledged her condolences with a

brief nod before asking, "How long have you worked with my husband?"

"Almost a year," Heather said. "I helped him with his classes and making notes with his research." She gave a crooked smile. "He was obsessed with the legend of the attack on Oahu."

"As was my father," Maliea said. "Did you work with him as well?"

"Only when they asked me to take notes," the pretty TA said. "And only after Taylor surfaced a possible clue to the whereabouts of the shipwreck. Your father did years of research on the topic." Heather's lips press together. "He didn't share the information he had. I was surprised when he invited Taylor along on the trip to the island."

"That might've been my fault," Maliea said. "I asked my father to make more of an effort to be a part of his son-in-law's life besides just being the department head." It was a lie. But Heather didn't know that. Maybe her father had taken Taylor with him to counsel him on fraternizing with students. "You were pretty close to my husband," Maliea said as a statement, not a question.

The woman glanced away. "Only as close as a student can get working with a professor for almost a year."

Heather wasn't going to admit to her affair.

"Yeah." Maliea lifted the box. "I'm done here." It

did no good to get angry now. Taylor was dead. He was gone. She didn't need to waste energy and emotions being angry that he'd had an affair with this TA.

Maliea had more important problems to solve. Number one, feeding and keeping a roof over her daughter's head. She prayed the insurance company would come through soon with what little money they had on the policy. It might help in the short term. Surely, there were scholarships for single mothers that would help them go back to school and get a degree. She needed something that paid more than her dancing gigs. She'd quit college when she'd gotten pregnant with Nani. Taylor had wanted her to stay home and raise their daughter.

While he'd had an affair with his teacher's assistant.

As she passed Heather, the woman turned with her. "Seems such a shame that your father didn't share information about the shipwreck so that others could continue the research. I don't suppose you know where he kept a journal…?"

A dozen retorts came to mind. Maliea bit down hard on her tongue before replying, "No idea." And she grabbed the photos of Nani from the table beside the door and laid them across the top of the box. She crossed the threshold, leaving her husband's lover standing in the middle of the office they'd shared.

Maliea marched down to Andrea's office, where Reid stood in the doorframe, his gaze going from the people in the office to Maliea as she approached. He stepped aside, allowing her to enter. "Find anything interesting?" he asked.

Maliea snorted. "Sure did." She laid the box on the floor beside Andrea's desk and took the photo frames off the top. "I left all the books in Taylor's office. I'd appreciate it if you could dispose of this box of his personal belongings. I don't need any of it."

Andrea stood, came around to the box and lifted the lid. "What do you want me to do with it?"

"Sell it, give it away," Maliea waved a hand, "burn it for all I care."

Andrea's gaze rose to meet and hold Maliea's.

Maliea's eyes narrowed. "Just don't give it to—"

Andrea nodded solemnly without saying a word.

Maliea tipped her head toward her father's office. "May I?"

"You bet." Andrea stepped aside. "There's not much to handle. Your father was a very neat man," her lips quirked upward on the corners, "although at times he was absent-minded. He said that if he didn't write things down, he'd forget them. He kept a journal of all his research and carried it everywhere."

Maliea's pulse quickened. "Did you find the journal among the things in his office?"

Andrea's shoulders drooped. "No. When he left that morning to catch the plane to Niihua, he had the journal with him. It went down with the plane. All they recovered was the black box and—" She clapped a hand over her mouth, her gaze shooting to the department head's office where Nani sat at her grandfather's desk, quietly coloring.

"—the bodies," Maliea whispered. That hollow feeling in her gut swelled, the incredible weight of her grief pressing down on her. She swallowed hard on the lump rising in her throat.

"Do they know what happened?" Andrea asked.

Maliea drew in a breath and let it out slowly to calm the rise of emotion that threatened to overwhelm her. She forced the words from her mouth. "Based on radio communications between the pilot and the ATC, the actuator had disconnected, making it impossible for the pilot to control the aircraft. The National Transportation Safety Board ruled the crash as an accident."

Channeling the anger she felt at losing her father, Maliea said, "Maybe it's just as well that the journal is at the bottom of the ocean. If my father had not been obsessed with the lost treasure of Red Beard, he might still be alive today."

"So true," Andrea said, her brow puckering. "I'm going to miss him around here. It won't be the same. We'll probably get some young guy with half the class." She smiled, her lips trembling. "It might be time for me to retire."

Maliea's eyes widened. "What would they do without you? You've run this department as long as I can remember."

"I'm too old to train a new department head half my age. I might as well open a daycare." Her smile brightened. "Would you consider me as a full-time babysitter for our little Nani?"

Maliea hugged the older woman. "In a heartbeat."

When Andrea stepped back, her eyes shone with unshed tears. "Now, get busy in your father's office before I embarrass myself."

Maliea glanced toward Reid.

"Do you want me to help?" he asked.

"Yes, please," she said softly.

Having only known this man for a few hours, she found herself leaning on his strength during this most difficult time.

She couldn't let herself get used to having him there. Eventually, she'd be on her own again.

In the meantime, she had a strong shoulder to lean on. A man who wouldn't be too busy having an affair with a pretty young Teacher's Assistant to look out for the wellbeing of a single mother and her child.

Yeah, he had incredibly broad shoulders. He was

also ruggedly handsome. A single woman in the prime of her sexuality could fall for a guy like that.

A shiver of awareness rippled across Maliea's skin as Reid followed her into her father's office.

CHAPTER 7

REID FOLLOWED Maliea into her father's office and came to stand beside her as she stared around the room. "Are you all right?" he asked.

She gave him a weak smile. "I just came face-to-face with the piece of work that kept my husband 'working' a lot of late nights at the office."

"Mama," Nani said from the chair behind the desk. "Come see my picture."

Maliea crossed the room, leaned over the desk, and stared down at the coloring book. Her daughter had been happily coloring in. "That's beautiful. I like the way you used blue for her hair."

"She has blue hair because she's a mermaid, like in Papa's story." Nani looked toward Reid. "Do you want to see?"

Reid crossed the room to stand beside Maliea. "That's very pretty," he said. "Are those seashells?"

Nani nodded. "Yes, sir."

"What is that behind the mermaid?" Maliea asked.

Nani looked up at her proudly. "I drew that," she said. "That's the gigantic mountain on the big island. Like in Papa's story."

Reid shot of glance toward Maliea, cocking an eyebrow.

Maliea shrugged. "My father made a whole book of short stories for his granddaughter. He read them to her every time he put her to bed. It became a tradition. When my father wasn't there, I read the stories to her from my father's hand-written storybook. He even had colorful drawings on the pages." She smiled sadly. "Until he wrote the book for Nani, I never knew my father was such a skilled artist."

Reid looked back at the mermaid with the mountain behind her. "Have you ever been to the big island?"

Nani shook her head. "Papa promised he would take me one day." Her brow puckered. "But my Papa isn't coming back. Is he?" Her gaze met her mother's.

Maliea swallowed hard as she shook her head. "No, sweetie. Papa isn't coming back."

"I'm going to miss Papa," Nani said.

The sadness in the little girl's eyes nearly undid

Reid. His heart hurt for the woman and her little girl.

Nani laid down the crayon and reached up her hands toward Reid.

Reid lifted the little girl into his arms without giving it a second thought. "Why don't we look out the window while your mama goes through some boxes?"

Nani laid her head on his shoulder and went with him willingly to the window.

Reid hated seeing the troubled eyes of a three-year-old. Obviously, she had loved her grandfather. If Maliea's words meant what he thought they meant, this little girl's father had been having an affair with his Teacher's Assistant. How could a man risk losing his family chasing some younger woman's skirts? Reid would have done anything to keep his family together.

"I want to go home," Nani whispered.

Reid's chest tightened. What did you say to a three-year-old whose home had been torn apart? "How would you like to come and stay at my cabin?" he asked.

"I'd like that," Nani said.

Reid's glance shot over the top of the little girl's head toward her mother.

Maliea stared across the room, her gaze connecting with his. "Are you sure?"

Reid gave a brief nod.

Maliea smiled weakly. "Thank you. It will give me a place to stay while I figure out what's next."

Reid stood for a long time at the window with Nani in his arms, her head resting on his shoulder. Holding Nani was how it had felt when he'd held Abby in his arms.

God, he missed her.

Nani's breathing became slower, and her body relaxed. She fell asleep like that.

Reid's chest swelled with a profound feeling of something so deep he couldn't put a name to it. It wasn't so much love as need, and not even that but a sense of rightness. Holding Nani, a little three-year-old girl, felt so right. At the same time, he had a twinge of guilt twisting his gut. He should be holding his own little girl. But that wasn't going to happen except during his court-ordered visitation. He wanted more time than that. He wanted his child in his life all the time.

Less than thirty minutes later, Maliea spoke, "I'm done here." She straightened from the box she'd been going through on the floor. "I can carry this box if you can carry Nani," she said.

"I'll get the box," Reid said, "if you want to take Nani."

"No use disturbing her," Maliea said. "Unless your arm is getting tired."

Reid said. "I'm fine." His arm could be aching

and nearly falling off, and he'd still want to hold the child.

Maliea lifted the box off the desk and carried it into Andrea's office. She loaded the photos of her daughter into the box and smiled at the older woman. "What I left behind, you can give away, throw away, or do whatever you like with it."

"Are you sure?" Andrea asked, her brow wrinkling.

"I'm sure," Maliea said.

Andrea touched her arm. "Just so you know, the professor loved you very much. You and Nani were his world."

Maliea snorted softly. "Maybe so, but not enough of his world to give up his obsession over fictitious treasure."

Maliea set the box on a chair beside Andrea's desk. Then she turned and hugged Andrea. "We'll be talking soon," she promised.

"Please do." Andrea's eyes filled with tears. "I lost your father. I hope I don't lose you and Nani as well." A single tear slid down her cheek.

"Don't worry. We love you," Maliea said. She bussed the older woman's cheek with a light kiss. "Let me know if you retire. We'd love to see you more often."

The older woman nodded and laid a hand on Nani's back. "Take care of our girl."

Maliea forced a smile. "I will." She held out her hands.

As Reid eased Nani into her arms, Maliea gathered her daughter close.

Reid lifted the box and carried it toward the door. They took the elevator down and left the building.

At the SUV, Reid stored the box in the back. Maliea helped Nani into the backseat and buckled her seatbelt. Then she slipped into the front passenger seat. Reid climbed into the driver's seat and started the engine. "Where to?"

Maliea sighed. "I might as well tackle my father's apartment. At the very least, I need to wrap my arms around what must be done."

While Reid pulled out of the parking lot, Maliea entered her father's address on her smartphone with a stop at the store where Tish had promised to leave Nani's car seat.

Using the map's directions, Reid wound his way through the streets of Honolulu, his gaze going to Maliea. He tried to gauge her reaction to the thought of going to her father's house to sift through his belongings. Reid's mother and father were still alive back in Texas, as were his two sisters and a younger brother. He didn't know how it felt to lose a parent or sibling. But he knew how it felt to lose a friend and then have to go through his belongings to pack and ship them back to family members. It hurt knowing that a friend or family member wouldn't be around. The good times they'd shared and the bad times they'd weathered together would be nothing more than memories.

Maliea stared out the front windshield, her teeth chewing on her bottom lip. "I don't know how *someone* will react when we get there." She tipped her head toward the backseat.

"I'll do what I can to distract her," Reid assured her.

Maliea faced Reid briefly and gave him a weak smile. "It's hard." She choked on her words, tears welling in her eyes.

Reid reached across the console, took her hand in his, and gently squeezed it. "I'm sorry you have to go through this."

"I know you didn't sign on for this kind of duty," she said. "But it's easier for me, knowing I'm not alone. So, thank you."

Reid gently squeezed her hand again. He didn't know what else to say. So, he didn't say anything and just held her hand. The more he held it, the more he liked how it felt. She had slender fingers, but they were solid and competent. Yes, she was hurting, but she wouldn't let that detract from being an excellent mother to her daughter. She would protect her from the bad guys as well as her own sadness. Reid admired that. Maliea was a woman who would remain resilient for the people she loved.

He'd like to know more about her comment concerning her husband's Teacher's Assistant, but he didn't feel he had the right to pry. If she wanted him to know more, she'd tell him. Based on the fact she'd left all her husband's belongings with her father's secretary, Reid would guess that Maliea had no love lost for her dead husband. She seemed much closer to her father.

Maliea pointed to the next corner. "Turn in there. This is the store where Tish said she'd leave Nani's car seat."

Reid pulled in. They found the car seat in a shopping cart in a cart corral, quickly transferred it to the SUV and settled Nani into the safety belts.

Back on the road, it wasn't long before Reid pulled in front of a white, stucco apartment complex near the university.

Maliea unbuckled her seatbelt and looked up at the building before her. "When I married Taylor, my father sold the house I grew up in. He said he didn't need all that room and preferred to live closer to the university. I think the empty house got to him. After my mom passed, he had me to keep him from getting lonely. That all changed when I married and moved out. I think the memories in the house were too much for him."

"I can understand," Reid said. "I wouldn't want

to be alone in the same house that held only memories of my wife and daughter."

Maliea shot him a grimace. "I'm sorry. I should be more sensitive. You've lost family members, too. Maybe not in death, but it still hurts."

Reid pushed his door open. "It's been a couple of years. The pain fades."

"You must've loved her a lot," Maliea said softly.

He paused before getting out of the SUV. "Looking back, I don't know that I loved her as much as I loved the idea of being a family."

As soon as he said the words, he wished he could take them back. He'd never told anyone as much as he'd just told Maliea. Maybe it was because, for the first time, he'd admitted it to himself. Or perhaps it was because misery loved company.

No, it was more than that. This woman loved her child and would do anything to protect her. She'd also loved her father dearly. He suspected her relationship with her husband had not been the best, but he'd also bet that she would have stuck with the man if only to provide a stable family life for her daughter.

As Reid came around the vehicle, Maliea was already out of her seat, had the back door open and Nani's harness unbuckled. She lifted the sleeping child into her arms. "Could you carry that box up to my father's apartment? I'll leave it with his other things until I know more about what I want to do for a place to live and what I want to do with his belongings."

"Can do." Reid opened the rear hatch of the SUV, gathered the box in his arms and closed the hatch. He followed Maliea inside the building and down the hallway, where she stopped in front of a doorway halfway along the corridor.

Maliea fumbled in her pocket for her keys, balancing Nani on one arm.

The door just past her father's opened, and an older woman poked her head out. "Oh, Maliea, have you come to get the rest of your father's things?" The woman emerged into the hallway, wearing sleek white trousers, a navy-blue top, gold bangle bracelets and fuzzy slippers. Her short gray hair was neatly slicked back from her forehead, and she wore bright red lipstick.

Maliea turned to the older woman, her key in her hand. "Not today, Ms. Jennings. I just came to get an idea of what I need to do."

The woman's eyebrows rose. "Oh, I thought you might be coming for the remainder of the items that you didn't have moved yesterday."

Maliea's body stiffened. "What do you mean? I didn't have anything moved yesterday."

Ms. Jennings' brow wrinkled. "The people from the moving company took several boxes of your father's things and packed them into a small moving van. When I asked them what they were doing, they showed me an invoice indicating they would move his things that day. Didn't you send them?"

Maliea shook her head. "I didn't order any boxes to be moved. Did they say what company they were with?"

Ms. Jennings frowned. "I can't recall. They showed me the invoice briefly. I didn't make note of the actual company."

"Were they wearing uniforms?" Reid asked.

Ms. Jennings nodded, her brow still wrinkled. "The men were wearing white coveralls and baseball caps. I don't recall seeing any company logo on the coveralls. They carried empty boxes in and left a short time later carrying what appeared to be full boxes. I wasn't around for the better part of the afternoon because I had an appointment with my hairdresser. I assumed they got everything moved until you showed up."

Maliea pushed the key into the lock, twisted and shoved the door open. She drew in a sharp breath. Her gaze shot to Nani's face. The three-year-old was sound asleep, her head on Maliea's shoulder.

Reid set the box of Maliea's father's things against the wall in the hallway and stepped past Maliea into the apartment. The place was a shambles. The living room sofa lay on its back, the cushions flung aside with massive rips down the middle and an empty bookshelf sprawled across the entryway. Reid went quickly through the apartment and returned to where Maliea stood in the hallway. He shook his head. "Not good."

Maliea swore under her breath.

"Oh, sweet Jesus," Ms. Jennings said behind Maliea as she peered over the younger woman's head into the apartment.

"Ms. Jennings, could you describe, in more detail, the men who came to the apartment?" Reid asked.

The woman shook her head. "They both wore baseball caps and white coveralls. One guy was tall, almost as tall as you." She tipped her head toward Reid. "The other guy was much smaller. What I could see of his facial features were kind of young or feminine. But I didn't get a real good look at his face."

Reid glanced down at Maliea. "Does this apartment complex have a video monitoring system?"

Maliea shrugged. "I don't know."

"It doesn't," Ms. Jennings said, her lips pressing into a thin line. "I've been after facilities management for months about installing a video monitoring system for this place. They still haven't. Perhaps this will convince them."

Reid backed into the hallway. "We need to

report this to the police." He pulled his phone from his pocket and entered 911.

The dispatcher answered within seconds.

Reid gave him the address and stated his emergency. The dispatcher assured him that a unit was on its way and would be there in approximately five minutes. He ended the call and waited with Maliea in the hallway.

Ms. Jennings, with her nice outfit and fuzzy slippers, stood with them wringing her hands. "I wish I had known they weren't a moving company. I would've paid more attention. It just made sense for a moving company to come in and pack his things. Isn't it bad enough that he's dead? Why did they have to come and steal his things?" She hugged her arms around her body. "Is there any place safe from bad people?"

"Not everyone's bad," Maliea said softly. Her hand moved up and down on Nani's back.

Thankfully, the three-year-old remained asleep.

A pair of police officers entered the building and joined them at Maliea's father's apartment.

Nani's eyes blinked open and widened when she saw the police officer standing beside them. She lifted her head. "Why is there a policeman here?"

Maliea smiled at her daughter reassuringly. "They came to tell us how sorry they were that Papa was in a plane crash."

She met Reid's gaze. He nodded.

Maliea stepped away from the doorway and out of view of the disaster.

After Maliea and Nani were out of earshot, Reid spoke softly with the officers, explaining the situation, careful that Nani couldn't hear his words. All the while, he half-listened to what Maliea was saying to her daughter.

"So," Maliea forced another smile for her daughter, "how do you feel about spending the night camping out in Mr. Reid's cabin?"

"Yes, please!" Nani's face brightened.

"Then that's just what we'll do," Maliea said cheerfully, although she felt far from happy.

Ms. Jennings stood at her father's doorway, staring inside.

"Aren't we going into Papa's apartment?" Nani asked, pointing at the doorway she recognized.

Maliea shook her head. "No, sweetie, Mr. Reid is just going to go inside with the police officers and make sure everything's all right. Then we can go to Mr. Reid's cabin. They'll only be a minute."

Reid's glance swept both ends of the hallway before he led the police officers into her father's apartment.

Because he didn't like leaving Maliea and Nani out in the hallway for long, he made quick work of showing the officers around, giving them the few details he knew and the fact that the owner of the apartment had died in a plane crash. The officers made notes and promised to follow up with fingerprints.

"You might want to speak with the neighbor, Ms. Jennings. She saw the men who came. She said that they removed several boxes before she had to leave. By the looks of it, they emptied the bookshelf in the entryway, the one on the other side of the living room, and everything in and on his desk."

The lead officer made notes as Reid spoke.

Impatient to return to Maliea and her daughter, Reid hurried through what he knew and ended his discussion with, "Now, if you'll excuse me, I need to make sure Professor Hasegawa's daughter and granddaughter are okay. Please lock up when you leave and let us know if you find anything." He handed a card to one of the officers. "You can reach me at the number on the card."

Reid emerged into the hallway to find Maliea halfway to the other end. She'd set Nani on her feet and held her hand. When Nani saw Reid emerge from her Papa's apartment, she pulled her hand free of her mother's and ran toward him.

Reid met her halfway to keep her from getting close enough to the door to see inside her grandfather's apartment. He didn't want her to be upset by the mess inside. Reid swung her up into his arms and kept walking toward Maliea. "Ready?" he asked.

Maliea pressed her lips tightly together. She

turned, led the way back to the parking lot, and waited while Reid tucked Nani into the backseat and buckled her belt. After he closed the door, he met her gaze.

"If the offer is still open," she said softly, "we'd like to stay at your cabin tonight."

He nodded. "The offer is open. You're more than welcome." He opened her car door for her and waited for her to slide into the passenger seat. Once she settled, he closed her door, rounded the front of the SUV and slid into the driver's seat.

"Are we camping in your cabin?" Nani asked from the backseat, clapping her hands excitedly. "I've never been camping."

"You've never been camping?" Reid asked. "Sleeping in a cabin is not exactly camping, but one of these days, I'll take you on a real camping trip. With a tent and a campfire."

"Yay!" Nani called out. "We're going camping."

Maliea shook her head. "For tonight, we could pretend we're camping by putting up a sheet like a tent. We can eat popcorn and tell stories."

Nani's eyes widened. "That'll be so much fun!" she exclaimed. Then she asked, "Can Mr. Reid sleep in our tent?"

Maliea's cheeks turned a soft shade of pink. "If he wants to."

"Do you want to?" Nani asked, her gaze meeting his in the mirror.

"Sounds great," Reid said. Again, he thought about everything he'd wanted to do with his daughter Abby and might never get to. He had her for such short bursts of time. Nani would love Abby, and Abby would love Nani. Maybe someday the two could meet and play together.

Who was he kidding? Once Reid neutralized the danger, Maliea wouldn't need him anymore. He'd move on to his next client, and she'd forget all about him, as would Nani. It's not like they'd set up play dates for the girls. Although, the idea had merit. Now that he'd settled in Hawaii, he could have his daughter for at least two weeks during the summertime. It would be nice if she had a friend to play with.

He pushed thoughts of the future aside and focused on the present.

To keep her excited daughter occupied, Maliea dug into her purse and pulled out what looked like a kludged-together, homemade book. She handed it back to Nani in the backseat. "Here, read Papa's stories or at least look at the pictures."

Maliea straightened in her seat and stared out the front windshield. "I just don't know what's happening," she whispered.

"I don't know what your father had of value in his apartment. But it appeared as if they were looking for something in particular."

"Just like in mine," Maliea said softly.

"The empty bookshelves in the front entry and the living room struck me. They stripped your father's desk entirely."

Maliea turned toward him, her brow dipping. "My father had a lot of books, especially books about Hawaii. And his desk was always stacked with papers. Some of those papers could have been student dissertations or test papers he might have been grading. He wasn't the neatest man, but he had his way of organizing things. He had dozens of books and journals on the shelves."

"When was the last time you saw those papers and books?"

"Nani and I visited my father the day before his trip to the island." She pressed her lips together to keep them from trembling. After a moment, she continued. "His shelves were just as I remembered them. Every other time I visited, the shelves were full of books, journals, and notebooks. And his desk was stacked with papers. I can't imagine he cleared any of that before he left for that trip."

"Well, it was all gone," Reid stated.

"Why would they take all his books and papers?" Maliea asked.

Reid struggled to answer her question, but he had an idea. "When you were talking to Andrea at your father's office, she said your father kept a journal with all his notes from his interviews with Islanders about the Redbeard Treasure."

Maliea nodded. "Andrea said my father had his journal with him when he left. They found my father and Taylor but, as far as anyone knows, the journal is at the bottom of the ocean. My father didn't go anywhere without that journal."

"You know your father, and if he had it with him, you're right. It's probably at the bottom of the ocean."

"When I spoke with the Teacher's Assistant, Heather," Maliea said, "she mentioned that she worked with my father and Taylor, taking notes in their meetings. She also said that my father didn't share much about his research on the Redbeard Treasure."

"Would your father put that information on his computer at work?"

Maliea shook her head. "No. He kept his research on the Redbeard Treasure strictly on his time and the interviews and notes in his personal life. He would not use university time or equipment chasing down what most people considered only a legend, a piece of fiction found in a California newspaper."

"I think someone is hoping that your father made notes elsewhere. They took books and every piece of paper out of his office in case he stashed something away that could give them the clues they need. Maybe they hope to find his notes on the research he'd done so that they could go after the lost treasure of Red Beard."

"But who would know he'd been researching the treasure?" Maliea asked.

"His secretary, the Teacher's Assistant, people he interviewed on the various islands," Reid suggested.

Maliea frowned. "He's been searching for years. Ever since my mother died. I thought it was good for him to have something to occupy his mind. The research eased his grief. It gave him something else to think about—but he still made time for me and Nani.

"They trashed my apartment, my car and my father's place. Why haven't they trashed his office? Or Taylor's, for that matter?"

"I noticed the university hallways have video surveillance," Reid said. "That could've kept them from so blatantly tossing those locations."

"Surely, by now, they've realized I don't have my father's notes. Hopefully, they'll leave us alone."

Reid wasn't so sure. They had been pretty ruthless with the contents of both apartments, and they'd tried to drag Maliea under a car. To do what? Reid's mind went through several scenarios, and he liked none of them. "We don't know if they'll leave you alone. In the meantime, you can stay with me until we have a better handle on who is behind this and why."

He headed for the other side of Oahu, to the little cabin he'd rented for the duration of the Kualoa Ranch assignment, going over every detail he'd learned that day and coming up with no answers.

One thing was clear—he couldn't leave Maliea and Nani to their own devices. These people were dead set on finding whatever it was they were looking for and might not stop at stabbing sofa cushions.

CHAPTER 8

MALIEA STARED at the road ahead as they drove across the island, going over everything that had happened over the past twenty-four hours, from the break-in at her apartment to finding her father's apartment similarly trashed.

Now, she was heading to the tiny cabin she and Nani had holed up in earlier that day before they'd met the man Tish had insisted was a good guy who would protect them with his life.

After being with Reid for the better part of the day, she could understand why Tish trusted him and would send her friend and that friend's child to him for protection.

Reid appeared to be a man of grit, strength and integrity. A man she could trust.

Trust was something Maliea had a hard time giving, especially after the man who'd promised to love, honor and cherish her had cheated and had an affair with his Teacher's Assistant while lying to his wife about his whereabouts and activities.

She didn't even know why Reid had divorced his wife and left his daughter. Suddenly, knowing more about this man protecting her and her daughter seemed more important. How did she approach the subject?

Should she just ask him why he'd divorced his wife, or had it been the other way around?

Excuse me, Reid, did you get a divorce because you cheated on your wife?

Maliea shook her head. Too personal. The man was a bodyguard. What did it matter if he'd cheated on his wife? He wasn't Maliea's husband or even her boyfriend. All she should care about is that he kept her and Nani safe.

Still, she couldn't help being curious about the ruggedly handsome man who had their lives in his hands.

Maliea sighed.

"Why the big sigh?" Reid asked.

She started, her cheeks heating. "A lot going through my mind."

"Like what?" he asked.

"Crashes, break-ins, treasure hunters and lying cheaters," she said and wished she hadn't added the last.

Reid's lips twitched. "Did you know he was cheating?"

"I had a suspicion, but I was too busy working and taking care of our home and our daughter to dig deeper or dwell on it." Her lips twisted. "Turning a blind eye doesn't make it go away."

"True," he said, staring at the road ahead. "I understand the part about being too busy to see the signs. I was too busy being deployed one mission after another to slow down long enough to see the signs. One day, I returned home, and she immediately asked me to sign divorce papers."

Maliea's heart dipped into her belly. "Wow. That's harsh."

"I was naïve enough to think all was okay while I was out fighting for our country." He snorted softly. "I feel incredibly stupid that I didn't see it coming. She remarried within a month after our divorce was final. Abby thinks of her new husband as her real daddy. I'm just her bonus daddy who takes her on vacation every so often."

Maliea had started the conversation to get the answers she'd wanted. Now that she had them, she didn't feel any better. She hurt for the man who'd been selflessly defending his country while his wife had been screwing around on him. The worst part was losing his daughter to another man.

"I'm sorry."

Reid shrugged. "Don't be. I should've been more

attentive, provided more emotional support and been there for my daughter."

"You were serving your country," Maliea argued. "Surely, your ex-wife knew what she was signing on for."

"I don't think she really understood what it meant to be a military wife to someone in Special Operations and DEVGRU. We belonged to the Navy first, family second. She wanted to be first and found someone who could give her that."

As they left Honolulu behind, Reid kept glancing into the rearview mirror.

Maliea looked over her shoulder. "What's wrong?"

"I'm not sure," he said. "That car behind us has been following us since we left your father's apartment complex. Could be a coincidence."

Maliea looked back again, making note of the dark sedan trailing them by several car lengths. "What can we do to make sure?"

After another brief glance in the rearview mirror, he said, "Look ahead at the map and find me a neighborhood with a few streets. I want to see if the car follows us through."

Maliea opened her cell phone and brought up the map application. "There's a neighborhood ahead on the left. Slow down to make the turn."

Reid did as she suggested and turned onto a

street leading into a neighborhood with around a dozen different streets crisscrossing each other.

After they entered the little community, Maliea looked back. The sedan hadn't turned in to follow them. "Think he went on?"

"I'll zigzag through the streets for a few minutes to make sure," Reid said.

He made a right on the next street and a left at the following corner. Another left brought him to the road that had led them into the group of homes.

Maliea swiveled in her seat, looking all around for the dark sedan. "I don't see the car."

Reid slowed, looked both ways and into his rearview mirror and nodded. "Probably just a coincidence. Even so, keep an eye out in case he shows up again. We don't want to lead anyone out to the cabins."

"Right," Maliea said, on high alert for trouble. Reid might be used to watching over his shoulder, but this was new to Maliea. The situation felt so clandestine, like something you'd watch in a thriller movie.

By the time they reached the cabins, Maliea's neck ached from constantly looking behind them or checking for dark sedans coming out of side roads. She was ready to be safely tucked into Reid's cabin, which would lead to another set of anxieties that had nothing to do with bad guys chasing them. Those

ELLE JAMES

feelings would have everything to do with her unexpected attraction to the man and the close proximity of living with him in a one-room building.

When Reid drove past the cabins, Maliea twisted in her seat. "Aren't we going to the cabin?"

He nodded. "After we pick up something for dinner. I don't know about you, but I think Nani might be hungry and need to call it an early night. We can order a meal to go and take it back to the cabin to eat."

Maliea relaxed, glanced at her daughter in the back seat and smiled.

Nani lay with her head leaning against the side wings of the car seat.

Maliea was glad Reid had thought ahead about a meal for her daughter. She felt a little guilty that she hadn't and, even worse, had no money to purchase their meals.

"I'll pay you back as soon as I get paid," she said softly.

"Don't worry about it." He pulled into the parking lot at the diner and shifted into Park. "Let's just get something to eat and head back to the cabin."

"I can stay here with Nani while you order the food."

He shook his head. "I'll call in the order and wait with you. They can bring the food out when it's ready."

134

Maliea nodded. The man thought of every-thing. What a difference from Taylor. He'd expected her to do all the grocery shopping, all the take-out food ordering and make any appoint-ments necessary. He'd never offered to help other than to pick up an occasional loaf of bread on the way, grumbling that she hadn't taken the time to run to the store since she wasn't working a day job.

"Do you like working in Hawaii?" she asked in an attempt to fill the silence.

He nodded. "I wasn't sure I would, but so far, I do. The weather is nice, and there's a lot to do. It can get hot here, but not like it does in South Texas. At least we get rain and a breeze here."

Maliea smiled. "I love my home state."

"Have you ever lived anywhere else?" Reid asked.

She shook her head. "I can't imagine living anywhere I can't see the sea. It's in my blood... my heritage. I think that if I lived in a land-locked state, I'd feel trapped."

He nodded. "I can see that. The islands are beautiful, lush and green. We've had years of drought in San Antonio. It gets dry and dusty."

"I would like to visit other states," she said. "Someday. I want to see fall foliage and a real winter with snow. I've never seen snow, except in movies or the news. I think it would be great if

Nani could experience a white Christmas just once."

"We didn't get snow in San Antonio, either. At least not enough to even make a snowball. My folks used to take us on trips to New Mexico during our Christmas vacations. We got to play in the snow, sled down hills and learn to snow ski. We had to drive twelve or thirteen hours to get there, but it was worth it," he said with a smile. "I had hoped to take Abby someday when she was old enough. I think she'd like the snow."

Maliea nodded, staring at the building in front of her, thinking about the dreams she'd had when she, Taylor and Nani had still been a viable family. "We'll do those things eventually. I just need to go back to college, earn a degree and make enough money to support us and have some left over for travel."

Reid gave her a brief nod. "I believe you will. You seem to be very determined, and you care about your daughter."

"I'd do anything to make her happy and her life easier." She turned in her seat to glance at Nani. "She deserves a joyful life full of adventure and discovery. I should never have dropped out of college halfway through my junior year."

"Why did you?" Reid asked.

Maliea grimaced. "I got married and then pregnant soon after. We decided it would be best if I stayed home to raise Nani."

"We?" Reid asked gently.

Maliea glanced toward him briefly. "Childcare is expensive. Taylor had just finished his master's degree and landed a job as a teacher at the university. He didn't make enough money for me to pay for childcare while I completed my degree."

"The cost of living is high here," Reid commented.

She nodded. "It made sense for me to quit school and raise Nani. Only he didn't even make enough money for me to stay home full-time. We agreed that I could work nights as a hula dancer like I had when I was a single college student. The extra money meant we could afford diapers and groceries. He would be home at night to care for Nani when I went out to dance."

"How long did that arrangement last?" Reid asked.

"Until Taylor said he had to teach night classes or stay late to work with students who needed additional tutoring. Or so he said." Maliea looked away, embarrassed that she'd been naïve enough to believe his lies. "My father and my friends helped by watching Nani on the nights I danced. I put Nani in a mother's-day-out program when I worked at a local supermarket stocking shelves or working as a clerk."

"I take it you did a lot of juggling," Reid said.

Maliea nodded. "But enough about me. So, home for you is South Texas?"

"It was," Reid answered. "I grew up there."

"Have you been back often?" she asked.

"Not very," he said. "Not since I joined the Navy fourteen years ago."

"Don't you like Texas?"

He shrugged. "I go back occasionally to visit my parents and siblings, but I don't miss the heat in Texas."

"Do you like Hawaii and think you'll stay? Or will you eventually go back home to Texas?"

"I hadn't decided. I was glad to land a job after leaving the Navy. It's hard to get work when all you have on your resume is weapons training and combat experience. When Hawk offered us work here, we jumped on it."

I hope you stay.

Maliea almost said the words aloud but clamped her lips closed before she could.

Jenny from the Burger Bar came outside just in time to keep Maliea from blurting out anything else that might sound stupid or needy. She carried a sack full of food and handed it through Reid's window with a friendly smile. "Enjoy!" she said with a wink and flounced back into the restaurant.

Reid handed the sack of food to Maliea.

Her round of questioning ended, Maliea sat

silently as Reid shifted the SUV into reverse, backed out of the parking space and pulled out onto the highway. The sun had set with a brilliant display of red and orange as it slipped below the horizon.

Maliea marveled at the stunning display of nature. She never got tired of the beauty of her island.

A few minutes later, Reid parked behind the cabin.

Nani woke as the lights blinked on inside the SUV. She yawned and stretched as Maliea helped her out of the car seat and carried her to the cabin.

Reid grabbed the sack of food and hurried ahead to unlock the back door.

Before Maliea could enter, three men surrounded them.

Reid spun and crouched, ready to spring.

Maliea clutched Nani close, her heart beating fast until she recognized two of the men as Logan and Rex, Reid's teammates.

Reid recognized them a few seconds sooner and cursed under his breath. "Don't sneak up on me like that unless you want to end up in a hospital."

"Dude," Logan said. "You're getting slow."

"I heard you coming," Reid grumbled.

Rex chuckled. "And you were going to take us out with a bag of Burger Bar food?"

"It could be done," Reid assured him. He

reached out a hand to the man Maliea didn't recognize. "Jones, good to see you. Did you draw the short straw?"

The man he'd called Jones grinned. "On the contrary, I drew the long straw. I've been looking forward to spending some time on Oahu. Just want to know if I'm working Kualoa with these two boneheads or taking over for you…?"

"Let's get inside," Reid said.

Rex frowned in the light from the stars beginning to appear overhead. "Worried about something?"

"Maybe," he said and unlocked the back door.

When Maliea started to go in first, he touched her arm. "Wait."

She nodded and stood still, holding Nani close.

Reid entered, switched on the light inside and was back out a moment later. "Clear."

The three men surrounding her waited for her to go in first, then followed her up the steps and into the small cabin.

With all four men inside with her and Nani, Maliea almost felt claustrophobic.

"About time you got home," Logan said. "We've been waiting for you."

Reid set the sack of food on the table and turned to face the others. "We had business to take care of at the university and at Maliea's father's apartment."

Reid swept a hand between Maliea and the new guy. "Maliea Kaleiopu, Jackson Jones. He's another one of the Brotherhood Protectors."

"Nice to meet you," Maliea said.

"Pleasure's mine," Jones responded and then all focus turned to Reid.

Maliea worked on laying out food for Nani, hoping her daughter wouldn't be disturbed by Reid's briefing of his teammates.

Reid told them about sorting through the two university offices and then arriving at her father's apartment to find it had been treated similarly to Maliea's.

Maliea was glad he'd left out all the details that might upset Nani. Fortunately, her daughter was hungry and dug into the chicken strips and macaroni and cheese Reid had ordered for her.

Even though Nani appeared focused on the food in front of her, Maliea knew her daughter. She was smart and listened to everything going on around her, taking it all in.

When Reid finished his short briefing, Rex asked, "So, what's it to be for you, Kualoa or bodyguard duty?"

Maliea breathed a sigh that Reid's teammates seemed to realize having a child in their midst meant keeping the information they shared to a minimum or shared in an abbreviation or code.

She understood what they were asking, but

Nani probably wouldn't. Still, Maliea held her breath. Reid had a choice of handing Maliea and Nani off to the new guy, Jones, and going back to the security detail at the film production site on the Kualoa Ranch. Or he could continue to provide protection to her and Nani.

Reid stared down at Nani, happily biting into a crispy, fried chicken strip. Then, his gaze went to Maliea. For a long second, he hesitated.

It was the longest second of Maliea's life.

"Bodyguard," he finally said.

Maliea released the breath she'd been holding, her chest filling with air and hope.

Logan clapped Jones on the back. "If you love rogue cattle, sneaky teenagers and sweating, you're gonna love the ranch."

Jones clapped his hands together. "I've done a little research on it. Sounds amazing. Some of my favorite movies were filmed there."

"Like Jurassic Park and King Kong?" Rex asked.

Jones grinned. "Those along with Pearl Harbor and Fifty First Dates."

Rex met Reid's gaze. "Well, with that settled, we'll leave you to your meal. If you need anything, let us know. We're only a shout away."

"Thanks," Reid said.

After the men left the cabin, Maliea felt she could breathe again. So many large men in one tiny room was a bit overwhelming.

"You could've passed us off on Jones," Maliea said softly.

Reid shook his head. "Couldn't."

"Why?" Maliea asked.

Instead of answering, Reid opened the bag and dug out one of the wrapped hamburgers. "Let's eat, shower and get some rest. I'll take the sofa. You and Nani can have the bed. And, for the love of Mike, don't argue."

"Who's Mike?" Nani asked.

Maliea laughed, a feeling of relief washing over her. She and Nani were beginning to get to know this man and felt safe with him around. That went a long way in Maliea's books after everything that had happened.

She hoped he'd be around long enough for them to figure out what was going on and who was behind it. Until then, she couldn't let down her guard. Not even with this man she might foolishly be starting to trust.

CHAPTER 9

REID ATE his burger while studying Maliea as she worked with Nani to ensure the child ate enough to fill her little belly.

Nani was tired and cranky, ready to lay down and go back to sleep despite her short naps in the SUV getting to the cabin.

Maliea barely touched her sandwich, too wrapped up in taking care of her little girl. The dark circles under her eyes gave testament to the lack of sleep she'd had in the past two days.

Once satisfied that her daughter had eaten enough, she gathered her into her arms and carried her into the little bathroom. Fifteen minutes later, they emerged. Nani was bathed, her long dark hair combed and braided down her back. She wore an oversized T-shirt that hung down to her ankles.

She ran to Reid and held up her arms.

Reid lifted the little girl and inhaled the scent of innocence, his heart pinching hard in his chest. "Hey, cutie. You smell like popcorn."

She frowned. "Do not. I smell like shampoo. Mama washed my hair."

Reid made a show of sniffing her hair again. "I believe you're right. You do smell like shampoo. How smart of your mother to wash your hair with shampoo and not popcorn."

Nani giggled. "You don't wash your hair with popcorn. That would be silly."

"Is it?" he asked, raising his eyebrows. "Then I better stop washing mine with popcorn."

Again, Nani giggled. She hugged his neck and planted a kiss on his cheek. "I like you, Mr. Reid."

He smiled down at Nani, his heart fuller than it had been in a long time. "I like you, too, Nani."

"Can you tuck me in?" she asked.

"I'd be honored," Reid responded and carried her to the bed, laying her on the side furthest from the door. He pulled the sheet and light blanket up to her chin and tucked it loosely between the mattress and box spring. "That feel all right?"

She nodded.

Before he could straighten, she wrapped her arms around his neck and hugged him tightly. "Good night, Mr. Reid."

"Good night, Nani," he said, holding onto the hug a little longer.

When he let go, she turned to her mother. "Mama, will you read to me from Papa's book?"

Maliea held up the book. "Wouldn't miss it," she said. "Should I start at the beginning?"

Nani nodded and yawned. "Yes, please."

Maliea opened the handmade book carefully to the first page. "A long time ago, there was a little girl who lived in the Gathering Place."

Nani pointed at the page. "That's Oahu and that's Honolulu," Nani said proudly. "Papa told me."

Reid's heart swelled at the picture the mother and daughter made. With Maliea sitting propped against a pillow beside her daughter, holding the book lovingly made by Nani's grandfather.

Maliea was an amazing mother. Patient, kind and blessed with a heart of gold.

"One day a man with a red beard came to the Gathering Place on a ship with huge masts. He pretended to be a friend to the king and all the people," Maliea continued. "But once he got inside the king's palace, he stole all the king's gold."

Nani's eyebrows formed a V over her pert little nose. "He was a bad man."

Maliea nodded. "Yes, he was. His other men went through town stealing from the people who lived there."

"Why didn't they fight the bad men?"

With a shrug, Maliea said, "They didn't know

they were bad men at first and didn't have anything to defend themselves."

Nani glanced at Reid. "They needed Mr. Reid to help them."

"Yes, they did," Maliea said with a smile. "Only Mr. Reid wasn't there. He wasn't born yet.

"The man with the red beard and all his men took the gold and riches, carried them out to their ship and sailed away from the Gathering Place. The people of the island never saw them again."

Nani lay back on the pillow with a yawn. "That's sad."

"It's just a story," Maliea said. "Close your eyes and go to sleep thinking of happy thoughts about mermaids and seashells."

Nani yawned again, her eyes drifting closed. "Read the next..." Before she finished her sentence, Nani was asleep.

Maliea continued to sit beside her daughter for a couple minutes more and then slipped off the bed. She leaned over Nani and pressed her lips to her daughter's forehead. "Ko'u aloha, my darling."

Her fingers brushed the loose hairs around her daughter's cheeks behind each ear. With another smile at her daughter, Maliea straightened and turned to Reid. "Is it all right if I get a shower?"

He nodded. "Of course. I'll watch out for Nani."

"Let me know if she wakes up. I'll try to make it short," Maliea said.

"Take your time," Reid said. "She'll be fine with me."

Maliea hesitated a moment longer, then gathered a T-shirt, panties and gym shorts out of the bag she'd dragged from her apartment to Tish's and now to the cabin. After one more glance at her daughter, Maliea disappeared into the small bathroom.

No sooner had the door closed and the shower was turned on, then Nani's eyes blinked open. "Mama?"

Reid came to stand beside the bed and took Nani's hand. "She's in the shower. What do you need?"

Nani rubbed eyes with her knuckles. "I want her to read some more from Papa's book. It helps me sleep."

Reid glanced from the book on the nightstand to the little girl blinking up at him. He wasn't sure how long Maliea would be in the bathroom. "I can read to you," he said, almost regretting the words as soon as they left his mouth.

A slow smile spread across Nani's face. "Will you?"

The girl was precious and out of her element, maybe even scared. Reid couldn't help himself.

He took the book in his hands and carefully opened it.

Nani tugged on Reid's jeans. "Not up there," she

said through a big yawn. "Here." She patted the bed beside her. "So I can see."

Reid sat on the edge of the bed and held the book out to Nani. "Where did you and your mother stop?"

Nani turned the pages past the first story and stopped at the second. "Start there."

Reid studied the handwritten words for a moment before reading aloud.

"Not long after, the messenger came to the king on Oahu to share the news about the ship with the big white masts visiting the Big Island, just such a ship appeared in the bay of the Gathering Place. The ship's captain had a red beard, just like the one the messenger had described. He came ashore to greet the king. The king had a huge luau prepared and invited the ship's captain into the palace." Reid glanced down at Nani, certain she would be asleep by now.

Her eyes were wide, staring up at him.

"Want me to keep reading?" he asked.

She nodded and slipped her hand into his free one.

Reid squeezed her fingers gently and continued to read, "The red-bearded captain and some of his men joined the king in the palace. He ate the food, watched the dancers and visited with the king. When the luau was over, and the captain and his men got up to leave, they turned on the king and took him, hostage. Then they stole all the king's gold."

Nani's eyebrows formed a V over her pert little nose. "He was a bad man."

Reid nodded. "Yes, he was." He continued, a little worried the story would keep Nani awake rather than lull her into a deep sleep. "What the king didn't know was that the captain was the famous pirate, Redbeard. While Redbeard was stealing the king's gold from the palace, his other men took all the riches from the people who lived in the village. They even robbed the little girl's father, stealing the gold and jewels he'd acquired from visitors who'd come to the island before."

"Why didn't they fight the bad men?" Nani asked.

With a shrug, Reid said, "They didn't know they were bad men at first and probably didn't have anything to defend themselves."

Nani glanced up at Reid. "They needed you to help them."

He smiled down at the child's innocence. "Yes, they did. Only I couldn't be there. I wasn't even born yet."

"I feel sorry for the little girl and the people of the Gathering Place," Nani said.

"Me, too," Reid agreed. He continued to read. "The man with the red beard and all his men took the gold and riches, carried them out to their ship and sailed away from the Gathering Place. The people of the island never saw them again."

Nani lay back on the pillow and closed her eyes. "That's sad. The king was nice to him."

"Yes, he was."

"That wasn't nice of the captain to take his gold," Nani whispered.

"No, it wasn't," Reid said softly. "But it's just a story." When she didn't respond, he sat for a moment longer, staring down at Nani's sweet face. Her dark lashes made little feathery crescents against her cheeks. The sheet rose and fell over her tiny chest as she breathed slowly and deeply.

Afraid to move and disturb the child in her sleep, he stayed where he was and continued to silently read the story, admiring the drawings Professor Hasegawa had painstakingly drawn for his granddaughter.

The story went on to tell of how the little girl was sad and vowed to search for the ship and the pirate who'd stolen her father's treasures. She wanted to bring everything back to the Gathering Place and to the people they belonged to.

She ran to the water's edge and spoke with the mermaids along the shore, who told her the ship had sailed with the winds, moving southwest toward Garden Island. Because they hadn't followed the ship, the mermaids couldn't be certain where the ship had gone next.

As Kanani stared out at the night sky, a storm blew in from the northeast with powerful gusts that pushed her into the water.

The mermaids helped her back to shore and told her to seek shelter until the storm passed or she would be swept out to sea.

Kanani returned to her home, hunkered down and waited until the winds died down. The next morning, the sun came up over the Gathering Place. Many homes had been flattened or swept away by the powerful winds. She helped families whose homes had been demolished and tended to children while the adults worked hard to rebuild what had been destroyed.

When she finally went back to the sea, it was calm, but the ship was nowhere to be seen.

Too young to sail on her own, Kanani couldn't follow the ship's path. She waited, pacing the shore, asking visitors from the west if they'd seen the ship with the huge masts that looked like clouds and a hawk's head carved into the bow.

Each time she asked, she got the same answer. No one recalled such a ship.

As the days passed, she despaired of ever finding the ship and Redbeard, the pirate.

The little girl grew older and taller, learning how to sail with the wind, going further and further from the shore. One of her village elders taught her how to navigate by the stars. When

Kanani was older and strong enough, she left her village, climbed into her canoe with a sail she'd fashioned herself and set off to find the ship with the hawk's bow and the treasure Redbeard had taken from her people.

Her first stop was the Garden Island. Years had passed since the pirate ship had sailed away from the Gathering Place. She talked with many people, describing the ship, the night and the captain. One after another, they shook their heads. They hadn't seen a ship but remembered the ferocity of the storm that had flattened homes and swept their canoes out to sea.

About to give up, a woman stopped her. "Go. Speak with Old Man Rangi, the man on the hill. He sees everything."

Kanani climbed the hill overlooking the windward side of the island. There, she found an old man weaving a basket made of palm fronds as he stared out to sea.

"Old Man Rangi, do you remember the night of the big storm so many years ago?"

The old man nodded. "I lost my wife to the sea that night."

"I'm so very sorry," Kanani said. "Did you see a ship pass in the night during that terrible storm?"

Old Man Rangi's eyes narrowed as he looked out at the calm waters. "The night my wife was swept away, I saw something in the distance. As she disappeared beneath the waves, a flash of lightning lit the sky. A ghost ship appeared with huge white sails and a carving on the bow in the shape of a bird's beak." He turned to look at Kanani. "As I live and breathe, I swear the ship had come to claim my sweet Noelani, to carry her away to the land beyond."

Kanani was sure the old man had seen Redbeard's ship. "Did the ship land on the Garden Isle?"

The old man shook his head. "The storm tossed the ship, sending it on toward the Forbidden Isle. Recovery from the storm was delayed by another storm the next night. Though my people tried to stop me, I paddled my canoe to the island a few days later, hoping to find the ship and my Noelani."

Kanani touched the old man's shoulder. "And did you find them?"

His fingers stopped their weaving motion. "The people of Niihau refused to talk to me and threatened to throw me off the island if I didn't leave on my own."

"Did you leave?" Kanani asked.

The old man stared down at his motionless hands. "I couldn't leave until I knew the truth. I asked one more man if he knew what happened to the ship. He was so angry that he and several others carried me to my canoe and tossed me in. As they pushed me out to sea, a small girl swam out to me carrying a pineapple to give me strength for the journey home. As she clung to the side of my canoe, she whispered, 'The ship ran up on the rocks in the storm. Everyone on the ship was swept out to sea.'"

"No survivors?" Kanani asked.

The old man shook his head. "She didn't say. I assumed none."

"And the ship?" Kanini asked.

He shrugged. "I didn't see it. I assume it was swept out to sea with the storm that hit a day later."

A sound pulled Reid out of the storybook. He glanced up to find Maliea standing in the doorway of the bathroom, her damp hair combed smoothly back from her forehead.

"Did Nani wake?" she asked in a whisper.

He nodded. "I read more of your father's story to her." Reid's lips twitched on the corners. "I admit, I got caught up in it and kept reading after she fell asleep. Your father was quite the storyteller."

Maliea nodded. "He liked to incorporate his research in the stories he told Nani. I told him he should write books and publish them. Other children might love the stories as much as Nani."

"This story is obviously based on the pirate Redbeard and the treasures he stole from Oahu." Reid frowned down at the handmade book in his hand. "Do you think all of the story was based on his research?"

"Sure. I'd bet some of it is based on his research. It's a fact that he interviewed people whose ancestors had passed down the legend of the theft on Oahu and the big storm that caused so much damage."

"And the sighting of the ship passing Kauai in the night?" Reid asked.

Maliea's brow furrowed. "Yes."

Reid pulled his cell phone from his pocket and searched the internet for Kanani Akamu. The name appeared in an article written by Joe Akamu, who claimed to be the great-great-grandson of Kanani, a woman who'd lived through the pirate raid of Honolulu and the great storm that had almost wiped Honolulu off the map around the same time.

Reid shook his head.

"What?" Maliea came to stand near him.

"Kanani Akamu was a real person who lived in Honolulu at the time of the great pirate raid and the storm." He looked up into Maliea's eyes. "Your father must have read about her in this article by the woman's great-great-grandson." He held out his phone for her to see the article.

As Maliea read the words, she frowned. "I always thought Kanani was a name he made up for Nani."

Reid searched the internet with the name of Old

Man Rangi. When nothing came up immediately, he added "1884" and "storm" to the search.

The name Ahe Rangi appeared in an article documenting the lineage of the Rangi-Manoa family from the 1800s through to modern-day Hawaii. Reid grinned up at Maliea. "Old Man Rangi was a real person as well." Again, he handed the phone to Maliea.

She read the article and sank onto the end of the bed. "My father's journal wasn't the only place he documented his research. He included it in my daughter's storybook." Maliea took her father's book from Reid's hand, her face paling. "Whoever ransacked both apartments was looking for something. Do you think they were looking for this?"

Reid's cell phone vibrated in his hand. He glanced down at the screen where Rex's name was displayed. The man wouldn't call him this late unless it were important. Reid answered the call on the first ring, "Bennet here."

"I went out for a jog an hour ago and noticed a car parked on the side of the road not far from the cabins," Rex's voice came through the line in a whisper. "It was still sitting there when I got back from my run. The boys and I sneaked out the back door to investigate. Seems the car is occupied, and the guy inside has some kind of equipment pointed at your cabin. By the looks of it, it could be a listening device."

CHAPTER 10

REID PUSHED TO HIS FEET, his hand tightening around his cell phone. "Are you sure?"

"As sure as I can be," Rex said. "The windows are heavily tinted, but I'm almost positive he's using a listening device, and it's aimed at your cabin."

"What?" Maliea stood and moved closer. "What's wrong?"

He pressed a finger to his lips. "Checking it out now," he said softly into the phone. Reid switched off the lamp on the nightstand, plunging the one-room cabin into darkness. He crossed to the front window and eased one of the blinds down far enough that he could peer out into the night.

As Rex had reported, a car sat on the roadside.

"I see it," Reid whispered into his phone.

Maliea came to stand close to him. She leaned

her body into his and peered through the gap in the blinds.

She smelled fresh, like shampoo. The T-shirt she wore did little to disguise the fact she wasn't wearing a bra.

Reid's groin tightened.

"Want us to pull him out for questioning?" Rex asked, reminding Reid of the situation outside the cabin.

Reid cupped his hand over his mouth and phone and whispered, "Get the license on the vehicle and call it in to Hawk. As for pulling him out, you don't know what else he might have inside that car. He could be dangerous."

"At the very least, we can shake him up and send him on his way," Rex suggested.

"Do it," Reid said. "I don't like the idea that someone could be eavesdropping on us."

"Going to do some movin' and shakin'," Rex said. "Out here."

Maliea leaned close and spoke softly into Reid's ear. "What's happening?" Her breath was warm and soft against his skin, stirring desire to life in Reid's veins.

He tried to focus on the vehicle outside the cabin, but to bring her up to speed, he had to position his mouth close to her ear and speak softly. "There's a man in that car with listening equipment pointed at this cabin."

Maliea sucked in a startled breath.

Before she could say anything, shadows detached themselves from the bushes and eased up to the back of the vehicle. Moving in sync, the three men leaned against the back bumper and bounced the car violently several times.

An engine roared to life, headlights blinked on, and tires spun in the gravel. The car shot out onto the highway and sped away into the night.

The men stood still for a moment as if watching the disappearing car. Then, as one, they turned toward Reid's cabin and hurried to the door.

Reid opened it as they arrived.

Logan, Rex and Jones entered. Jones closed the door behind them.

"Someone knows you're here," Logan said.

Reid wanted to pace, but the room was too small and full of people.

Maliea stood beside the bed, her gaze going from her daughter to Reid. A worried frown dented her forehead. "If we knew for certain they wanted the book, I'd give it to them, so they'd leave us alone," she said.

Logan, Rex and Jones turned to Reid.

"I thought you said Professor Hasegawa's journal went down with the plane he was in," Logan said.

Maliea lifted her father's book from the night-stand and held it up. "My father made my daughter a storybook using his research. It chronicles a young Hawaiian girl's search for Redbeard's pirate ship and the treasure he stole from Honolulu in 1884."

"Did she find it?" Rex asked.

Maliea shook her head. "The book was a work-in-progress. My father left empty pages at the end. He wrote more as he came up with new adventures and clues. He was on his way to Niihau based on what he'd learned on Kauai. It takes time to get permission to visit the island. The residents aren't very welcoming to outsiders. They never wanted to join the United States and prefer to be left alone."

"Do you think the people harassing you are after the clues that will lead them to the lost treasure of Red Beard?" Logan asked.

Maliea shrugged. "I can't think of any other reason my daughter and I have been targeted."

His three teammates fixed their gazes on Reid.

"You need to bug out," Rex said.

"And go where?" Maliea wrapped her arms around her middle. "I don't have money for a hotel or food. I have to work. If I can't leave my daughter and know she's safe, I can't work. If I can't work, I can't feed my daughter." She raised her hands in the air. "Trying to stay a step ahead isn't working." She brushed her hand over her daughter's head. "I'm worried for Nani."

Rex met Reid's gaze. "Take her to Hawk."

Reid's brow dipped. "Take who?"

"The child will be safer on the Parkman Ranch, surrounded by their security system, Hawk and other members of the Brotherhood." Rex nodded toward Maliea. "Both of you could stay at the ranch until the people following you are caught. I forwarded the license plate of the car to Hawk. I expect to hear back from him soon."

Rex's cell phone pinged. He glanced down at the screen. "It's Swede." He received the call and held the phone up to his ear. "What did you find?"

Maliea moved to stand close to Reid. "Who's Swede?"

Reid rested a hand on the small of Maliea's back and leaned close to answer briefly, "The technical guru for all of the Brotherhood Protectors. If it can be found on the internet, he's our guy." His attention immediately shifted back to Rex. Hopefully, Swede had something on the guy who'd been stalking them with his listening device.

THE WARMTH of Reid's hand at the small of her back gave Maliea a comforting sense of security. But that wasn't all it was doing to her.

She liked how large and strong his hand felt through her thin T-shirt. It made her wonder how it would feel to have that hand pressed against her naked skin. A shiver of awareness rippled through her.

"Are you cold?" Reid asked.

Far from it. Heat rose up her neck into her cheeks. "No. I'm fine." Like hell she was. She'd lost her husband in a plane crash not too long ago, and she was having lusty thoughts about a man she'd just met.

Did that make her a bad person?

Never mind, her husband had been sleeping with his Teacher's Assistant for the past year, and they hadn't had sex in all that time.

Maliea had thought that she'd lost all desire for making love since having Nani. She'd been too tired to even try after dancing at the luaus and events. Not that Taylor had initiated anything. She'd told herself their lack of a love life was because they were working so hard to make a living that they didn't have time for each other.

Any spare time Maliea had, she spent nurturing her precious daughter. Her own needs always came second or third if Taylor wanted her to run an errand for him.

Reid's hand remained on her back. Maliea didn't move away or ask him to remove it. Her blood was smoking through her veins for the first time in a long time. And it felt good.

Thankfully, the man couldn't read minds. How embarrassing would it be if he could?

Rex didn't say much but listened for a couple of minutes before nodding. "Roger. Let us know what you find." He ended the call and met Reid's gaze. "Swede ran the license plate. It traced back to a rental car company at the airport. He tapped into their database and got the name of Mark Laster."

Reid looked down at Maliea. "Does the name ring a bell?"

She shook her head. "No."

Rex continued, "Swede ran a background check on the man. He worked as a bouncer at the Big Wave Dive Bar in Waikiki."

Reid frowned. "Worked?"

"He applied for unemployment a week ago," Rex said. "The reason he gave was that he was laid off. Swede called the bar. The manager said he fired the guy for being too rough with one of the customers. The customer threatened to sue the bar. The only way they got the customer to reconsider suing was to fire Laster."

"Sounds like someone with anger issues," Logan said.

"Someone who could easily trash two apartments," Reid said.

Rex nodded. "Swede tapped into the Honolulu Police database and looked up the report on the two break-ins. They ran fingerprints against the national database. No match so far."

"Does Laster have a criminal record?" Reid asked.

"No," Rex said. "Swede's going to keep an eye on when that car is turned in to the rental company. Hawk will send someone out to dust for prints. He wants to compare the prints in the car to the ones lifted at the apartments. Swede's also tapping into Laster's bank account."

"Makes sense," Reid said. "How does a guy who's been fired afford a rental car?"

"And why would he employ listening devices to creep on a woman and her child?" Maliea asked.

"He was a bouncer," Logan reasoned. "Would a jobless bouncer have the funding or the smarts to afford that kind of listening apparatus?"

"What reason would he have to follow the woman and child?" Jones asked.

Rex's phone pinged again. "It's Swede, again." He answered, "'Shoot." He listened, nodded and said, "Interesting. I know you like to get all the goods, but feed anything you can find to us as soon as you find it. It might help us put the pieces together... Right... Out here."

Maliea held her breath, waiting for Rex to give them anything they could actually sink their teeth into.

"Swede got into Laster's bank account. The jobless bouncer received a sizable deposit three days ago from an offshore account based in the Cayman Islands."

"Someone paid him to do their dirty work," Reid said, his lips pressing into a tight line. "Was he able to locate the owner of the Cayman account?"

Rex shook his head. "Not yet. It's some kind of a corporate account that's buried in other accounts."

"He couldn't tell who authorized the payment?"

"No." Rex pocketed his phone. "It might take time to wade through buried accounts to get down to the actual owner."

"I'm glad Swede is on it. If anyone can wade through the bullshit, it's him." Reid's hand dropped from where it had rested on Maliea's back. "Right now, we need to get these ladies somewhere safe until we know a little more about who we're up against. So far, they haven't been physically attacked, but who knows how far Laster will go for the money he was paid?"

Maliea shivered. "Where can we go?"

"The Big Island," Reid said. "Rex is right. You'll be safest there. The Parkman Ranch has a state-of-the-art security system and plenty of people looking out for the owner and his daughter. It's the safest place in the state." He glanced at Maliea. "Are you good with that plan?"

Maliea wrapped her arms around herself, chilled despite the warmth in the room. "I want to keep Nani safe." She nodded. "Yes, I'm good with that plan."

Reid's phone chirped. He received the call and lifted the phone to his ear.

Maliea watched Reid's face, trying to guess what he was hearing based on his reactions.

"Hawk, did Swede give you a situation report?" Reid nodded. "Yes, sir. We can be at the airport in thirty minutes." He ended the call and met Maliea's gaze. "Hawk's sending a plane. It'll be at the Honolulu airport by the time we get there."

Maliea looked toward her daughter, squared her shoulders and said, "Let's go."

The men helped carry her trash bag full of her belongings out to the SUV and stowed it in the back.

Maliea scooped Nani into her arms and left the cabin, followed by Reid.

He stowed his duffel bag in the rear of the SUV and opened the back door for Maliea.

Maliea settled Nani gently in her car seat.

Her daughter's eyes blinked open briefly and closed again.

Maliea hoped Nani slept through the entire trip. Thankfully, her daughter was adaptable.

The drive across the island was made in silence. Logan led the way in Reid's sports car. Rex followed Reid and Maliea in his SUV.

They made it to the airport without incident and drove to the general aviation terminal.

As they passed through the terminal and stepped out onto the tarmac, a plane taxied to a stop.

A set of stairs unfolded from the side of the cabin-class plane, and a pretty, dark-haired woman descended, followed by a broad-shouldered man.

Reid met the man halfway to the plane and held out his hand. "Hawk, glad you could get here so quickly."

The man Reid called Hawk smiled at the woman. "It helps having a pilot in the family." He looked past Reid to where Maliea stood, holding a sleeping Nani in her arms. "You must be Ms. Kaleiopu."

"I am." With her arms full, Maliea was spared shaking hands with the man.

Hawk turned to the woman beside him. "This is Kalea, my wife and Parkman Ranch's very own pilot. Let's get you two on board and back to the Big Island. I'm sure you're tired and could use a good night's sleep."

Maliea nodded. "That would be nice."

Hawk stepped around Maliea and Reid and took Maliea's garbage bag, stowing it in the side of the plane along with Reid's duffel bag.

Kalea smiled at Maliea. "You might want to let

Hawk hold your daughter while you climb into the plane. He can hand her up to you once you're inside."

"I'll hold her." Reid stepped up to take Nani.

Maliea handed over her daughter and climbed up the steps into the plane.

Reid followed, carrying Nani up the steps and ducking low to avoid bumping his head.

Once inside, Maliea moved aside so Reid could settle Nani in the back bench seat. He buckled the seatbelt around her daughter's lap and motioned for Maliea to sit on the other side. Once Maliea was seated and buckled, Reid sat on the other side of her child.

Nani tipped over and leaned against Reid. He adjusted her so that she could rest her head in his lap, smoothing a hand over her dark hair.

He was so gentle and concerned for Nani's well-being that it warmed Maliea's heart.

Taylor had always left Nani's care and comfort in Maliea's hands, taking care of himself first.

Maliea was sad that Reid couldn't be with his daughter full-time. She couldn't imagine the heartache he suffered being away from his little girl.

Kalea slid into the pilot's seat, adjusted her headset and fired up the engine.

Hawk pulled the hatch closed and locked it in

place. He pointed to the headsets hanging on a hook on either side of the back bench seat and motioned for Maliea and Reid to put them on.

Hawk joined Kalea at the front of the cabin, sliding into the co-pilot's seat. Once he adjusted the headset over his ears, he gave Kalea a thumbs-up and settled back.

Maliea studied Kalea as she flipped through the pre-flight checklist. Her voice came over the headset as she called the ATC for clearance. They gave her instructions for where to taxi and finally gave her the go-ahead to take off.

Maliea hadn't been up that often in an airplane. To be this close to the pilot, where she could see and hear everything she did, was slightly unnerving.

The plane sped down the runway, gaining speed quickly. Then it left the ground, and Kalea flew it out over the water, following the ATC's instructions for altitude and vectors. Soon, they were heading for the Big Island, leaving the glaring lights of Honolulu behind.

Nani slept the entire way to Hawaii's biggest island.

It seemed they'd barely reached their designated altitude when the ATC gave Kalea directions to land.

Maliea looked at the ground ahead and didn't

see an airport or a runway. Her pulse quickened. She'd just lost her father and husband in a plane crash. Were they headed for the same fate?

Reid reached out his hand and held hers, gently squeezing.

Maliea held on, glad for his reassurance. The man had been a Navy SEAL, which meant he'd flown so often it was like riding in a car or bus. He didn't get nervous.

Clicking sounded in her headset, and suddenly, lights blinked, illuminating a runway ahead.

Kalea brought the aircraft down, kissing the earth so gently that Maliea barely felt the impact of the wheels touching the tarmac. She released the breath she'd held all the way down and inhaled deeply.

Reid didn't release her hand until the plane came to a complete halt and Kalea shut down the engine.

While Kalea performed her post-flight check-list, Hawk left his seat and dropped the hatch, lowering the stairs almost to the ground. He left the plane and waited at the bottom of the steps.

Reid unbuckled his seat belt and Nani's, gathered her into his arms and descended the stairs to the ground. No sooner were his feet firmly on the ground, he turned to extend a hand for Maliea, balancing Nani on one arm.

She took the hand and let him guide her to the ground.

Kalea followed Maliea. Once everyone was out of the aircraft, Hawk raised the steps, closing the hatch. He unloaded the trash bag and duffel bag from the storage compartment and locked the plane. He turned as a pair of headlights appeared at the other end of the landing strip.

A large black SUV pulled up beside them. An older man climbed out of the passenger seat, helped Hawk stow the bags and turned to envelop Kalea in a tight hug. "That's my girl," he said and kissed her cheek. "Safe and sound."

"Oh, Daddy. Tell me you didn't worry the entire time I was gone." She shook her head. "I have over a thousand hours of flight time."

He nodded. "I know. I know. But I don't think I'll ever get used to you flying."

"It's safer than driving in Honolulu," she pointed out.

The man nodded. "True, but I can't stop worrying about my baby girl."

Kalea's lips twisted. "I'm not a baby anymore."

"You'll always be my baby," her father said and turned to Reid and Maliea. "Are you going to introduce me to your guests?"

Hawk stepped forward. "Mr. Parkman, this is Maliea Kalieopu, her daughter Nani and Reid Johnson, one of our Brotherhood Protectors I've had positioned on Oahu since coming on board."

Reid balanced Nani on one arm and extended his hand, firmly shaking the older man's hand. "I've heard many good things about you and the Parkman Ranch. It's nice to finally meet you."

"Hawk's guys are always welcome," Mr. Parkman said. "The Brotherhood Protectors are an amazing group of men."

Mr. Parkman turned to Maliea, his brow dipping as he held out a hand. "Ms. Kalieopu, please accept my sincere condolences for the loss of your husband and father."

Maliea's eyes welled with tears. This man was about her father's age, reminding her of her loss even without his kind words. "Thank you, sir."

"Come on, let's get you to the ranch house so you can catch a few hours of sleep while it's still dark." He waved them toward the SUV.

Reid followed Maliea, carrying Nani as the child slept on his shoulder, barely stirring.

Now that they were on a different island, presumably safe for the moment, the stress and uncertainty of the day bore down on Maliea's shoulders, making every step a struggle.

When she tried to get up into the SUV, she stumbled and would have fallen if Reid hadn't reached out with his free hand and steadied her.

Once she had her feet firmly under her in the

back seat, she sat and slid across, making room for Reid to get in next to her.

Hawk folded the seat forward and held it for Kalea, who climbed into the back. He climbed in next to her.

Reid locked the seat in place and slid onto the bench seat, settled Nani between himself and Maliea and secured her seatbelt around her.

Nani moaned and snuggled against Maliea. She slid her arm around her daughter and eased her over to lay her head in her lap.

Her heart swelled with the love she felt for her child. She truly would hand over her father's storybook if it meant whoever was plaguing them would leave them alone. But would they? Or would they continue to stalk them, hoping they had more information than was in the storybook?

Maliea couldn't care less about the lost treasure of Red Beard and wished her father had never heard of it. He'd still be alive if he hadn't gone to Niihau that day, chasing clues. For all Maliea knew, he'd been on his way back with no more information than he'd started with.

The driver pulled away from the landing strip and took them to the main house on the Parkman Ranch.

Maliea had heard of the Parkman Ranch but had never been there. Even in the middle of the night, she could tell the house was huge, sprawling and amazing. The Parkman family had owned over one hundred thousand acres since the early 1800s. They were a primary source of beef for the Hawaiian Islands.

The driver pulled up to the front of the house with its massive double door. Lights burned over the entryway and inside, welcoming them with their warmth.

Maliea was so tired she could barely crawl out of the SUV. Thankfully, Reid carried Nani up the steps and into the foyer.

Once everyone was inside and the door closed, Hawk entered a security code into the panel on the wall. "You're safe here. We had a security system installed throughout the main house, and we have cameras posted on the corners of all the buildings and outbuildings."

"What if you want to get some fresh air or stare up at the stars?" Maliea asked, wondering if it was worth being so rich you weren't safe to leave your home.

Kalea's lips twisted. "We have a walled garden where you can get outside for fresh air. We don't arm the system during the daytime because there are so many employees looking out for everyone, plus the cameras with a guard manning the monitors twenty-four-seven. Your room also has a balcony you can step out on without setting off an alarm."

Maliea nodded politely. Was it a home or a prison?

"Come on, I'll show you to your rooms." Kalea led the way up a grand staircase to the second floor and down a hallway to the end. "I've put you in one of the suites with two bedrooms and a shared sitting room. Since Reid is your protector, he'll want to be close enough to help you should you need it."

Kalea pushed through a set of double doors into a beautiful room with beautiful wood floors, large, fluffy area rugs and a seating area big enough for half a dozen people. A door led off each side.

Kalea walked into one and flipped a switch, lighting the room from a beautiful chandelier hanging from the ceiling. The room had a king-sized bed decorated with a bright white comforter trimmed in a thick gold braid. The furnishings were modern yet comfortable, providing a peaceful haven.

Maliea eyed the bed, her body swaying toward it, ready to stretch across the mattress and relax.

Hawk appeared behind them, carrying the two bags. "If you're hungry, Ule left ham slices in the refrigerator and a loaf of bread on the counter in the kitchen."

"I can make sandwiches and bring them up if you're too tired," Kalea offered.

"No, please," Maliea said. "You need sleep, too.

Right now, I want to get Nani settled. If I get hungry, I'll find my way and make my own sandwich. You've done so much for me already." She smiled at the pair. "Thank you so much. I don't know what I would've done without Reid and his team."

Hawk slipped an arm around Kalea's waist. "Just so you know, if you need to do anything and want to leave Nani here, she'll be safe. Kalea and I will watch her."

"Oh, I couldn't ask you to do that." Maliea shook her head. "You've done so much and been so kind. I don't know how I could ever repay you."

"You can do it by letting us look after Nani." Kalea's cheeks reddened, and her hand rose to rest on her belly. "We need the practice."

Maliea's eyes widened. "Are you…?"

Kalea nodded. "I found out today. You're the first to know besides Hawk. I didn't want to tell my father, or he would have grounded me and made you take the commercial flight in the morning."

"What did you not tell me?" her father's booming voice sounded behind Kalea. "And why would I ground you from flying?" He entered the suite, his bushy brows forming a V over his nose.

Kalea turned to face her father. "Oh, Daddy, I didn't want to tell you like this. I wanted to make a special dinner and break it to you then."

Her father's frown deepened. "You're not

leaving the ranch, are you?" He glared at Hawk. "You can't take my baby away from the only home she's ever known."

Hawk held up his hands. "Sir, trust me, I wouldn't do that. It's a great place to raise children. I want our child to grow up here, just like her mother."

"Damn right. When you two decide to settle down and give me grandchildren, they need to live here, learn to ride horses and appreciate their heritage."

Kalea slipped an arm around Hawk's waist and leaned into him. "We want our child to grow up on Parkman Ranch, just like I did."

"Good," her father's frown eased. "As long as we all agree. Now, what's this big news you didn't want to tell me?"

Maliea almost laughed out loud. The man might run a multimillion-dollar operation, but he was missing the obvious with his daughter.

Kalea looked up into her husband's eyes. "You tell him."

Hawk dropped a kiss onto her lips first, then faced her father. "Sir, you're going to be a grandfather."

"Damn right, I am," Mr. Parkman said. "Soon as you two get busy and give me a grandchild."

Kalea shook her head. "Daddy, that's what we're

trying to tell you." A smile spread across her face. "We're going to have a baby."

Mr. Parkman stood for a moment completely gobsmacked, his jaw slack, his brow wrinkled. "Don't pull your old man's chain. This isn't something you joke about." His eyes filled with tears. "You aren't joking, are you?"

Kalea shook her head. "I'm three months along. We're having a baby in six more months."

Tears slipped down the older man's weather-worn cheeks. He brushed them aside and went to his daughter, pulling her into a tight hug. "Your mother would've been so happy."

She hugged him back, tears welling in her eyes.

Maliea blinked back tears of her own. When she turned to look for Reid, he was behind her, laying Nani in the bed and tucking the sheet and blanket around her. He bent and pressed a kiss to her forehead and straightened.

When he turned to find her watching him, he grimaced. "Sorry. It's a habit. I kiss Abby's forehead when I tuck her in at night."

"Please. Her father rarely showed her affection," she smiled at him, then at her daughter. "I find it endearing. You know...love me, love my daughter." When she realized what she'd said, her cheeks burned. "Not that I expect you to love me. It's just a saying. Forget those words that just came out of my mouth." She turned away. "I'll just slink back into the other room and pretend I don't exist. How embarrassing."

Hands gripped her shoulders from behind.

Reid turned her to face him. "Don't be embarrassed. You're tired, and you've had a rough few days. You're allowed to be a little confused."

She leaned her forehead against his chest. "Thanks."

"I've only known you a short while, but I've already noticed that there's a lot to love about you. Don't sell yourself short. And don't settle for a man who won't show you and Nani the kind of love you deserve."

Maliea looked up into Reid's eyes, her heart beating faster, her chest swelling with appreciation for this man who'd taken up the gauntlet to protect her and Nani. Taylor never would have spoken words like that to her.

Reid was nothing like Taylor, and he was just what she needed at that moment. She had to remind herself not to get too used to him. He was her bodyguard, not her boyfriend or lover. When she and Nani were safe again, he'd move on to the next client.

Don't get too attached to the man.

Reid pressed a brief kiss to her forehead. "Let's get a sandwich. You didn't eat your burger earlier."

"Are you sure she'll be all right?"

"She slept on the drive, the flight and the drive

to the ranch house without waking. I think she'll be all right for a few minutes. We can go down, make our sandwiches and come back up to eat them in the fancy sitting room if you like."

Maliea nodded. "I'd like that."

"Or..." he said with a dramatic pause, "we could eat them out on the balcony. If the stars are still out, I believe we'll have a view of Mauna Kea."

"I'd love that. I've never seen the mountain in the starlight." Seeing it with Reid would make it even more special.

Careful, girl. You're not looking for a man, and he's not looking for a package deal.

No matter how much she coached herself, she couldn't help the thrill of excitement coursing through her at the thought of star and mountain-gazing with the handsome Navy SEAL.

Maliea was getting in way too deep and far too fast. Had she been that starved for affection and attention?

Yeah.

And poor Reid just happened to be the first man to make her remember what it was like to fall in love.

She might as well get used to the idea that, when he left, he would have set a high bar for any other men. What were the chances of her, a woman with a small child, finding another man anywhere close to Reid's caliber?

For the time being, she couldn't resist his company and followed him down the grand staircase. She even giggled like a schoolgirl as they opened doors, searching the first floor until they found the kitchen. Wrapped in a blanket of care and concern, she would take all the scraps he was willing to throw her way until there were no more to throw. The man had awakened her to a world worth living in.

CHAPTER 11

REID MADE sandwiches while Maliea found drinks.

She chose two bottles of beer, found a bottle opener and popped off the tops.

After he layered ham, cheese and lettuce on bread, he slathered a layer of mayonnaise over the top slice of bread and laid both sandwiches on a plate, garnished with a healthy portion of potato chips.

He carried the two plates, and Maliea had the beer bottles as they climbed the staircase to the second floor and back to the suite Kalea had assigned them.

The first thing Maliea did was check on Nani.

Her daughter slept soundly, still curled up on the bed.

Maliea would sleep with her daughter, and Reid would have the room on the other side of the suite.

He hadn't stopped thinking about Maliea and how good it had felt to hold her and tell her she deserved to be loved. The kiss on her forehead had ignited a longing he'd thought long gone, never to return. When his wife had walked out on him and taken Abby, he'd sworn he would never trust another woman again.

Maliea threatened to break through his promise to himself and make him believe there was still a woman out there who would give more than she took. A woman who would care how he felt and embrace the love he had to give.

Lana had done nothing but take, take, take. When she'd been pregnant with Abby, she'd complained through the entire gestation period, blaming him for everything that didn't feel right. He'd done his best to make her comfortable, but he couldn't always be there.

She'd blamed him for deserting her when she'd needed him most. What she'd needed was someone to listen to her whine and complain. She'd had a relatively easy pregnancy with no major complications.

Reid had been helpful when he'd been home and sympathetic to her pain and needs.

Lana had played on his concern to the point she'd made unreasonable demands.

Reid had put up with it throughout, even when

she'd gone into labor. He'd done everything she'd asked and more, so aware of the effort it took to bring a baby into the world.

Still, he'd belonged to the Navy and had to deploy shortly after Lana delivered Abby.

He'd hated being away from his wife and baby daughter. But that was the life of a Navy SEAL. Lana had married him after he'd become a SEAL. She'd said she knew and understood the sacrifices families had to make for their SEALs to serve their country.

Ha!

Lana resented the military, claiming it made unrealistic demands on Reid and his family. She never had help raising Abby. While he'd been gone on a particularly long deployment, she'd informed Reid that she was divorcing him over an email. The woman hadn't had the decency to wait until he'd come back from a particularly difficult battle in which he'd lost half his team.

She hadn't asked him how he was or how he felt about the loss of his friends and teammates. Instead, she'd launched into everything that was wrong with their car, their house, their gardener and their neighbors.

Lana blamed Reid for the damage done to her pre-pregnant body. She'd used his money to pay for membership to the local gym with daycare facilities. She'd dropped Abby in the daycare and worked out for two hours a day.

That's where she'd met her next husband. A man who made a lot more money than a Navy SEAL. A man with a big bank account who could lavish gifts on his wife throughout the year and never deployed to foreign countries at a moment's notice for months at a time.

Lana had hired a personal trainer to help her get her pre-pregnancy body back in less than four months. She'd been even more beautiful than when Reid had met her at McP's bar in San Diego.

Of course, Martin Harrington, the CEO of a tech firm making a high six-figure annual salary, noticed her. And she'd noticed him. Reid would bet she'd targeted Martin as soon as she'd seen the Lamborghini he drove.

The man could give Lana everything her heart desired: a new, expensive car, a fancy house and unlimited spending power on his credit card.

She'd filed for divorce before she'd locked down Martin's adoration. He'd been happy to take her and Abby into his home and give them everything Lana thought they deserved.

Because Reid had seen so many of his team-mates go through divorces after deployments, he hadn't been surprised when Lana had hit him with the papers as soon as he'd returned from a mission in Afghanistan. He'd been at a low point in his life, having lost half his team in an IED explosion.

He'd left for Syria when Abby was only three months old and returned after her first birthday. She hadn't known him and had screamed when he'd come to take her for his court-ordered visitation.

Abby thought of Martin as her real father and Reid as a distant uncle who tore her away from her mother every month for a weekend and two weeks in the summer.

He followed Maliea through the suite to the French doors leading out onto the balcony with its cushioned loveseat and low metal table.

The seat was small enough that he couldn't keep his leg from touching hers.

Every time he leaned forward for the sandwich or beer, his shoulder brushed against hers. Each contact sent a spark of electricity shooting through him. He should have stood and moved away, but he couldn't.

The woman had him knotting on the inside, his muscles tense, ready to spring into action.

To do what?

Grab Maliea and kiss her soundly on the lips?

Run his hands through her hair and kiss her until they were both restless?

Sweep her up into his arms, carry her to the

empty bedroom and make love to her all night long?

Whoa.

Reid abandoned the last couple of bites of his sandwich and sat back in his seat.

What was he thinking? This was his client—a woman with a small child. A widow who'd only recently lost her husband. What kind of asshole was he to think of making a move on her?

"You're frowning quite fiercely," Maliea said, staring at his face, her own brow puckering. "What are you thinking about?"

"Kissing you," he said before he could rein in his tongue.

Her eyes widened, and she swallowed hard. "Seriously?"

He pushed to his feet and stood with his back to her, staring out at the stars, the mountain and anything but Maliea. "Sorry. I didn't mean to blurt that out. Forget I said it. You should get some sleep. I'll probably leave you here tomorrow and maybe follow your father's storybook to Niihau and find out whatever he discovered."

Maliea came to stand beside him without touching him.

It didn't matter. Her nearness sent his blood burning through his veins, headed south to his groin.

"If you're going to follow my father's storybook,

I'm going with you," she said softly, not making any mention of his other statement—the one about the kiss.

His fingers curled around the balcony railing in an attempt to keep him from pulling her into his arms and kissing her.

"You can't go with me," Reid said.

"Why?" Maliea asked.

"What about Nani?" he reminded her.

"You heard Hawk and Kalea; they want to look after Nani. They want to know what it's like to take care of a small human."

"You trust them with your daughter?" Reid asked.

"Do you trust them?" Maliea asked.

Reid nodded. "With my life."

"And Nani's?" she pushed.

"Absolutely," he said.

"Then I'm going with you," Maliea said.

Reid drew in a deep breath and let it out slowly. "Okay. We'll let them know in the morning. And only if Nani isn't freaked out by being left behind."

Maliea nodded. "Agreed."

When Maliea made no move to go back inside and rest for the next day's activities, Reid bit out, "Go. Rest."

"Why?" she whispered.

"Because we might have a long day tomorrow,

and you'll need the sleep," he said, still not looking at her.

"No," she said. "Why do you want to kiss me?"

He tipped his head backward, closed his eyes and gritted his teeth. "This discussion has no purpose. Go to bed."

Out of the corner of his eye, he could see Maliea shake her head.

"Fine," he said. "I'll go. Goodnight." He turned to leave, but Maliea stepped in front of him, blocking his path.

"I told you I was sorry I said anything. Don't make this anymore awkward than I already have," Reid said.

"I hope I don't." Maliea wrapped her hand around the back of Reid's neck, leaned up on her toes and pressed her lips to his.

That one kiss unleashed inside Reid what had been building all day and evening.

His hands gripped her hips. Instead of pushing her away, he pulled her closer, deepening the kiss until she opened to him.

Reid thrust his tongue past her teeth to claim hers in a sensuous caress.

Both her hands wove into his hair, urging him to get even closer.

His hips moved against hers.

Her leg slipped up the back of his calf, her sex

sliding across his thigh, the heat burning through his jeans to his skin.

He lowered his hands to the swells of her ass and lifted.

Maliea wrapped her legs around his waist, her sex rubbing the ridge beneath the fly of his jeans.

He groaned into her mouth, his body on fire, his need all-consuming.

When he finally came up for air, his breaths were ragged as if he'd been running uphill. He set her back on her feet and leaned his forehead against hers.

"This is so wrong," he said.

Her hands lowered to rest against his chest. "Because I'm a new widow?" she asked. "Is it wrong for me to want to be desired after living with a man who chose his Teacher's Assistant over his wife?" Her fingers dug into his shirt. "Is it wrong to act on a passion so strong I can barely breathe?"

Reid's breath caught and held at the rawness in her voice.

She tipped her head up and captured his gaze with hers. "Do you really want to kiss me?" She sighed. "Because I really want to kiss you."

"I do," he said, weaving his hands into her thick dark hair. "But I'm afraid."

Maliea laughed breathily. "You're not afraid of anything."

He stared down into her dark eyes, holding her head steady in his hands. "I'm afraid that once I start kissing you, I won't be able to stop. I'll want more. Already, I've stepped over the line. This is wrong."

"Fuck the line," she whispered, digging her fingers into his shirt and pulling him closer. "Fuck what's wrong. Fuck me."

She reached for the button on his jeans, flipped it free and lowered the zipper.

Reid sucked in a sharp breath as his cock sprang free into her hand. "What about Nani?" he said softly.

Maliea shot a glance toward the open door of the other bedroom.

Reid could see Nani's small form exactly where he'd left her. Sound asleep.

"She'll sleep," Maliea assured him. "Or is it that you don't want me?" She started to back away.

Reid swept her up in his arms, carried her into the empty bedroom and set her on her feet. "Are you sure?"

"Never more certain in my life." As if to prove her point, Maliea pulled her T-shirt up and over her head, tossing it to the side. Then she reached behind her and unclasped the hooks on her bra.

Reid was there to capture her breasts in his hands as her bra slid to the floor.

Maliea's back arched, pressing her breasts into his palms.

For Reid, there was no going back. He wanted this. He wanted her.

While Maliea kicked off her shoes and shoved her jeans over her hips, Reid toed off his boots, dug a condom out of his wallet and shucked his jeans.

Maliea stood in front of him naked, beautiful and too tempting to resist.

He gathered her close and bent to kiss her. As it deepened, he walked her backward until the backs of her legs bumped into the bed.

"Sit," Reid said into her mouth.

Maliea responded immediately, dropping to sit on the edge of the bed.

Reid nudged her knees apart and stepped between her legs. His hand kneaded her breasts, pinching the tips of her nipples.

Then he dropped to his knees, his hands sliding down her chest to her inner thighs.

He parted her folds, his gaze locking with hers.

Maliea's eyes widened, and her breathing grew ragged.

When he bent to take her clit into his mouth, Maliea moaned and clutched the back of his head, urging him to take more.

He sucked her there, then flicked his tongue across the bundle of nerves making her jerk and writhe in response.

Her hips rocked to the rhythm of his tongue. The more he flicked, the more she rocked until her body tensed, and she caught and held her breath. "There—" she gasped. "Yes—there."

One last flick and she clamped his head between her knees, her body pulsing to her release.

Reid continued to lick her clit until she collapsed against the mattress, her fingers swirling jerkily around the nipple of her right breast. For a moment, she breathed in and out, regaining some of her composure. Then she sat up, scooted backward on the mattress and pulled him up with her.

Reid climbed up her body, settling his hips between her legs. He lowered his head to claim her lips in a long, hard kiss. It was good but not nearly enough to satisfy the desire swelling in him, turning his cock rock-hard.

"You can tell me to stop, and I'll respect that," he said, closing his eyes to focus on controlling his urges.

She reached up and cupped his cheek. "Look at me."

He did.

"I want this," she said clearly. "I want you. Please...make love to me."

The condom he'd fished out of his wallet lay on the bed beside Maliea. She reached for it, tore it open, fit it over the tip of his shaft and rolled it down to the base.

Her fingers on his dick nearly made him come before he'd even gotten started.

She guided him to her channel with one hand, cupped his ass with the other and brought him home.

She was so tight, so hot and wet, Reid couldn't catch his breath.

Maliea pushed him away until the tip of his shaft was all that was inside her. Then she pulled him to her, hard and fast, repeating the process several times until he took over.

Reid rocked his hips, driving into her over and over, gaining speed with each thrust. Soon, he was pumping like a piston in a race car.

The more he fucked her, the closer he came, rising to the edge where he teetered for a moment, holding back as long as he could to savor every second of their connection.

He flew over the edge, his release rushing through him, his shaft throbbing against her channel all the way to the end.

Still buried deep inside her, he dropped down onto her, loving the feeling of his naked skin against hers. Wrapping his arms around her, he rolled them both onto their sides and held her close for several more minutes.

She kissed his lips, his chin, his neck.

He kissed her eyes, her nose, her mouth and sighed. "What just happened?"

She lay against the sheets, a sleepy smile curling her swollen lips. "We proved we're alive." Maliea brushed her fingers against his cheek. "Don't worry. No strings attached. This doesn't have to mean anything more than a physical release. Nothing else has changed." She smiled up at him. "Now sleep."

He stared down at her, wondering if she'd lost her mind.

To Reid, everything had changed.

CHAPTER 12

MALIEA HAD NEVER SLEPT SO well. For a few hours after making love with Reid, they lay in bed, cocooned in each other's arms, skin to skin.

She'd never felt so protected, satisfied and cherished as she did wrapped in Reid's embrace.

Yeah, it might only be for one night. She'd promised him no strings and wouldn't expect him to make what they'd done anything more than what it was—one night of incredible, life-changing sex.

In the wee hours of the morning, Maliea left the bed, dressed in a long T-shirt and panties, and crossed the sitting room to check on Nani.

Her daughter slept on, unaware of the earth-shattering change in her mother's world.

As Maliea stared down at her daughter, Reid joined her, dressed in boxer briefs. He slipped an

ELLE JAMES

arm around her waist, drew her body close to his and kissed her temple.

They didn't say anything, just stood there looking at Nani.

For the first time since she'd given birth to Nani, Maliea could imagine what a real family would be like. She'd always provided the nurturing love and care for her daughter. Taylor had rarely contributed anything close to love and concern.

Yet, this man she'd known for such a very short time had shown her and her daughter more compassion than Taylor had in the three years of Nani's life.

She could already sense how sad it would be when her troubles were resolved, and Reid went on to his next assignment. He had no reason to remain in their lives.

Pushing any future sadness aside, Maliea basked in the warmth of his body next to hers and the strength of his hand resting against the small of her back.

For the moment, she chose to pretend this fantasy was real. It gave her a brief burst of happiness when she'd been so mired in grief.

They returned to the other bedroom and crawled beneath the sheets.

Reid pulled her close, spooning her against his body, holding her gently in his arms.

Maliea fell asleep, warm, sated and desired.

. . .

SUN STREAMED through the windows of the French door, warming her face and nudging her awake.

She rolled onto her back and stretched out her arm, expecting to encounter a muscular body in the bed beside her. When all she touched was bunched sheets and a pillow, she opened her eyes and stared at the empty space beside her.

Maliea sat up and quickly scanned the room. She swung her legs over the side of the bed and pushed to her feet, listening for the sounds of movement from the other room. The door to the bedroom was almost all the way closed.

No sounds came from the sitting room or the other bedroom.

She pulled open the door and hurried to her daughter's bedroom, where she found an empty bed, neatly made.

"Nani?" she called out as she crossed the bedroom to duck her head into the adjoining bathroom.

There was no sign of Nani or Reid. Any other time, Maliea would be concerned about her missing daughter. Knowing Reid was looking out for her calmed any fears.

A high-pitched squeal caught Maliea's attention. She went to the French door and stared out through the panes to a barn resting on a gentle slope a hundred yards away from the house and the people between them.

Nani held hands and skipped between Kalea and Hawk as they walked up the hill toward the house. She grinned and laughed at something Kalea said.

Reid followed close behind, a smile lifting the corners of his lips.

Having agreed to go with Reid to follow the clues in her father's storybook, Maliea was relieved to see how happy Nani was with Hawk and Kalea.

Anxious to get moving and find a way to the islands her father had visited in his research, Maliea hurriedly changed into jeans and a mint-green pullover shirt that clung to the curves of her breasts. It was one of her favorites, and she always felt sexy wearing it. Not that Taylor had ever noticed.

She'd bet Reid would.

Shoving her feet into her hiking shoes, she grabbed a swimsuit from the trash bag, a change of clothes and underwear and stuffed them into the small backpack she'd salvaged from her apartment. Not knowing how long they'd be gone, she added a toothbrush, toothpaste and a hairbrush.

Satisfied she was prepared for a possible overnight excursion, she descended the staircase, arriving at the bottom in time to hear her daughter's happy voice coming from the direction of the kitchen.

Maliea found Nani, Reid, Kalea, Hawk and Mr. Parkman in the kitchen. A short man, wearing an apron and wielding a spatula, scraped fluffy yellow scrambled eggs into a large serving bowl.

Hawk carried the bowl to a large kitchen table set with six place settings. He laid the bowl between platters of pancakes and bacon. A basket of toast, jars of various jellies and a small pitcher of syrup rounded out the selection of food.

Hawk smiled at Maliea. "Just in time for breakfast."

The man in the apron set a large pitcher of orange juice on the table.

Hawk waved a hand toward the man. "Maliea, this is Ule, the ranch cook. Ule, this is Maliea, and I believe you've already met Nani and Reid."

Ule nodded. "I have. Welcome to Parkman Ranch. Sit. Eat before it gets cold."

Everyone gathered around the table, including Ule, and took seats. Reid helped Nani into a chair between himself and Maliea and then held Maliea's chair as she settled into it. His hand brushed her shoulder briefly, sending a rush of heat through her body.

Images of his hands exploring every inch of her body send more heat rushing up her neck into her cheeks. She settled her napkin across her lap. "I'm sorry I slept in. Did I miss anything?"

"Not at all," Hawk said. "Reid said you needed the rest, so he brought Nani down."

"We took Nani down to the barn to help us feed the horses." Kalea smiled across the table at Nani. "She was a big help."

"I petted Dante's nose," Nani announced, excitedly. "His lips tickled my hand." She held up her hand.

"Don't worry," Kalea said. "We washed up as soon as we got back to the house."

"Aunt Kalea and Uncle Hawk are going to teach me how to ride a horse," Nani said.

"Only if your mother is okay with it," Kalea reminded the child.

Nani looked up at her mother, her eyes rounding, pleading. "Can I? Please?"

"We'll be very careful," Kalea said. "We will only lead her around an enclosed corral on one of the gentlest mares."

Maliea frowned. The thought of her tiny daughter on top of a huge horse scared her. "Nani's really small. Is she too young to learn now?"

Mr. Parkman let out a bark of laughter. "Kalea learned to ride before she learned to walk. I had her on a horse as soon as she could sit up on her own."

Kalea nodded toward Hawk. "She'll have both

of us making sure she doesn't fall off. Hawk grew up on a ranch stateside. He's as experienced with horses as I am. But if you're uncomfortable, we'll find something else to do."

Maliea looked down at her daughter, who stared up at her with her big brown eyes. How could she say no? She nodded. "You can learn to ride."

Nani squealed, stood in her chair and threw her arms around Maliea's neck. "I'm going to ride a horse."

Maliea smiled and hugged her daughter for a long moment. Then she settled her back in her seat. "You'll need to eat a good breakfast. Riding takes a lot of energy." She loaded Nani's plate with a single pancake and a spoonful of scrambled eggs. After pouring gooey syrup over the pancake, she reached for a small pitcher of milk and poured some into Nani's cup.

Nani struggled with her fork and knife to cut off a piece of the pancake.

Reid leaned over from the other side and cut the pancake into small pieces.

Maliea filled her plate with eggs, toast and bacon.

"Reid tells us you're going to follow your father's clues in his research of the lost treasure of Red Beard," Hawk said.

Maliea nodded as she chewed on a bite of toast.

"Since I'm staying with Nani today," Kalea said, "I contacted a pilot friend of mine who can fly our seaplane out to Niihau. However, you'll have to get permission from the chief of the community out there to visit the island. I've heard they aren't keen on visitors, and it can take time to get them to agree to let you land on the island."

"I'll see if I can pull some strings to get you in," Mr. Parkman said. "We supply their beef. It may or may not help convince them."

"My father was just there. I assume he was invited. You could tell them I'm retracing his footsteps before the plane crash. Maybe they'll feel sorry for my loss and let me in."

"I'll do that," Mr. Parkman said.

After they finished breakfast, Mr. Parkman went to his office and called the Niihau community's leadership. Kalea coordinated with the pilot.

Hawk took Reid to the Brotherhood Protectors' offices to outfit him with a satellite phone. When they returned to the ranch house, Hawk volunteered to take Nani out to feed the chickens.

Maliea carried her backpack out to the porch, ready to leave as soon as arrangements were finalized. Her gaze followed Nani and Hawk out to the chicken coop. Hawk held Nani's hand as she danced alongside him, probably talking his ear off.

The image made Maliea smile.

Reid joined her, carrying a similar backpack to

the one she'd packed. He dropped it on the porch and came to stand beside her.

"So, we're picking up where my father left off…?" Maliea asked.

Reid moved his head slowly from side to side. "I got to thinking about Mark Laster, the guy listening in on our conversations in the cabin. I read most of the storybook out loud. If he caught it all, he might be on his way to Niihau now."

"I'm worried about the people there. This guy, and whoever he's working for, might not be as considerate as my father in his pursuit of the treasure. I knew my father, and he wasn't interested in the riches so much as the heritage. He loved Hawaii. Our family has lived on these islands for centuries. He would have wanted to preserve the treasure for future Hawaiians to see and enjoy."

Reid's lips twisted. "I'm sure the people who trashed your apartment and his aren't nearly as altruistic."

"I shudder to think what they will do to anyone who gets in their way," Maliea said softly.

"Okay, folks," Mr. Parkman's booming voice sounded behind them. "Looks like you've got an official invite to Niihua."

Maliea spun, her pulse quickening. "We did?"

The older man nodded. "I spoke to the owners. The beef angle did nothing to impress them. When I told them Professor Hasegawa's daughter wanted to visit, they were quick to approve. Your father must have made quite an impression on them. The owners are sending a message to the island as we speak to let them know of your arrival."

"Thank you, Mr. Parkman." Maliea hugged the man's neck. "You've been so helpful and kind." She stepped back, letting her arms fall to her sides.

The old man's face stained a ruddy red. "Oh, well now, it was just a phone call."

"Niihau was the last place my father was seen alive," Maliea whispered, her eyes filling with tears.

Mr. Parkman laid a hand on her shoulder. "I was so sorry to hear of his plane crash. I'd heard of your father and some of the good things he did to help preserve Hawaiian heritage. He was a good man."

Maliea nodded, blinking back ready tears. She was saved from trying to speak past the lump in her throat when a voice sounded behind her.

"They're pulling the seaplane out of the hanger now." Kalea emerged from the house, tucking a cell phone into her pocket. "Should be topped off with fuel and ready to go by the time you get to the landing strip."

"I'll take you there," Mr. Parkman said.

"Thank you," Maliea said. "I can't tell you how thankful I am for all you've done for me and my family. I hope someday that I can pay you back."

Mr. Parkman shook his head. "No need. We're

one big community on this strip of islands. We help each other the best we can." He waved a hand. "Come on, let's get you on your way. I always thought the lost treasure of Red Beard was nothing more than a fairytale. I'm interested to know how this treasure hunt turns out."

Maliea wanted to know the same. The treasure had been lost over a hundred years ago. What were the odds it had survived the horrible storm?

A shiver of excitement rippled through her. Were they about to find out what had really happened to the lost treasure of Red Beard? If it existed, there were people who might be willing to do anything to claim it as their own. Her excitement turned to a bone-cold chill.

They needed to warn the people of Niihau that trouble could be on its way.

Hell, it might beat her and Reid there.

CHAPTER 13

REID, seated in the co-pilot's seat, spoke to Maliea throughout the flight from the Big Island to Niihau on the opposite end of the archipelago.

"I've never landed on the water in a plane," Maliea said softly into her mic.

Reid chuckled. "Then that makes two of us. As a Navy SEAL, I trained on this island while on active duty. We trained with helicopters and zodiacs. And we didn't interact much with the locals."

"It was probably just as well," their pilot said. "The predominant language is Native Hawaiian. The one to two hundred people who live here are believed to be full-blooded Hawaiian."

"Did your father speak the Hawaiian language?" Reid asked.

"Yes. He was fluent," Maliea said.

He glanced back at her. "And you?"

She nodded. "My mother's mother only spoke Native Hawaiian. My mother's first language was the same. She had to learn English when she went to school. She and my father made certain I learned the language of our people. They didn't want to see their culture die."

"I hadn't considered the language differences," Reid said. "Especially when everyone speaks English on all the other islands. People tend to be more receptive to you if you meet them in their own language on their own ground."

Maliea's lips pressed together. "I hope my skills aren't so rusty that I'll embarrass myself."

"You'll be fine," Reid said. "I'm sure they'll appreciate the fact you're trying."

It was late in the afternoon when their pilot landed in a sheltered cove dotted with fishing boats. The plane came in low and slow, landing on a surface as smooth as glass.

As soon as the propellor stopped, Reid climbed out of his seat and dropped down on the skid.

Two men rowed out to the plane in a canoe decorated with garlands of flowers. Each man wore a beautiful leafy lei around his neck.

Reid steadied himself on the plane's floats and reached up to help Maliea out.

When the canoe reached them, the man in the bow said something in Hawaiian.

Maliea responded, bowing her head slightly in

respect. She turned to Reid. "They want us to get into the boat. They'll take us to shore and to the village elders."

Reid gave a similar nod of respect and stepped down into the boat. Once he was steady, he helped Maliea in. She settled onto a wooden seat.

Reid eased onto the one behind her. The man in the bow turned on his seat, removed the lei from around his neck and placed it around hers. He said something in Hawaiian.

Maliea responded, speaking softly, fingering the green leaves. She turned slightly in her seat to look back at Reid, her eyes filled with tears. "They want you to have the other lei."

Reid turned to the man in the stern and let him transfer the lei from around his neck to Reid's. He inhaled, admiring the fragrant scent the leaves gave off.

Maliea explained. "These leis are made of the leaves of the maile vine. It represents the sorrow and respect for a cherished member of the community who has passed. It's a great honor that they considered my father a cherished member of their community." Her words choked with emotion as several tears slid down her cheeks. "They are taking us to the village. Their people have prepared a special feast in honor of my father's passing."

"How did they have time to prepare?"

Maliea gave him a weak smile. "They've been

planning it since they heard of my father's plane crash. It just happened to be scheduled for today. I think that's why they were so quick to let us come."

The two men dug their paddles into the water, turning the canoe around and heading for the shore.

Kalea had worked it out with the pilot to drop them off and return the next day to pick them up. Once the canoe was far enough away from the plane, the engine roared to life. Moments later, the plane sped across the water and rose into the air.

Looking forward, Reid noted the group of people gathered along the wooden dock, dressed in their finest Native Hawaiian outfits.

The women wore colorful dresses with crowns and wristlets of bright green leaves or flowers. The men were shirtless with long red loincloths, green bands of leaves around their ankles and their dark skin tattooed with tribal images.

They helped Reid and Maliea out of the canoe onto the wooden dock and layered more leis around their necks. They led their guests up a hill to a village adorned with flowers and leafy garlands.

Every man, woman and child had gathered. They greeted Maliea like a returning member of the family, guiding her to a prominent position in front of the leaders of their community.

The old man Reid guessed was in charge took her hands in his and spoke in a deep, rich voice.

Maliea nodded and responded in his language.

The leader waved a hand, and the crowd dispersed, going back to whatever preparations they'd been assigned.

The leader of the community led Maliea and Reid around the village, pointing out the highlights of their traditional existence, from the carefully tended fishnets to the construction of a new canoe. He went on to take them through one of their homes, proud of the electric lights powered by their array of solar panels.

Maliea translated as much and as fast as she could. "The island is owned by Keith and Bruce Robinson, the great-great grandsons of the original owner who first inhabited the island and vowed to preserve the cultural heritage of its people. To do that, they limit visitors."

Reid was always amazed at the resilience of the very young. Children ran and played like children all over the world, unaware of the differences in their lives versus the lives of other children on neighboring islands.

Maliea went on with her translation. "The island has no paved roads. Its people get around on foot, horseback or bicycles. They don't have running water or indoor plumbing. They gather rainwater from their roofs. The lack of amenities also limits the number of people who can live on the island. They have no doctor and no phones or internet."

"Have you told him about Mark Laster and the potential of others coming to their island in search of the Redbeard Treasure?" Reid asked.

Maliea shook her head. "When he's finished with the tour, I'll let him know."

The sun slipped lower on the horizon by the time the community leader brought them back to the center of their village. Once again, all the inhabitants had gathered. Tiki torches were lit, providing a hazy glow of light around the circle.

The scent of roasted pig made Reid's stomach rumble. He was glad he and Maliea had eaten a big breakfast as they hadn't stopped for lunch.

Once they were all in attendance, the community leader sat on the ground. Everyone who wasn't helping prepare the feast sat as well.

Villagers brought out platters filled with traditional Hawaiian delicacies like poi, fish, chicken, sweet potatoes, pit-roasted pig, breadfruit and other things Reid couldn't identify, but he vowed to try everything.

Maliea leaned close to the leader and spoke softly.

He listened without interruption. When she was done speaking, he nodded and said something.

Maliea turned to Reid. "I told him about Mark

Laster and the people we suspect employed him to help them find the treasure. He understands. They've had treasure hunters invade their island over the past hundred years, searching for the lost ship and the treasure that was stolen from Oahu."

"Did you tell him these people could be very dangerous?" Reid asked.

She nodded. "I did. He said no one has ever found the treasure on the island. They will fail as well."

Maliea spoke to the elder again, leaning close. Her concern and compassion were evident in her expression and the way she looked around at the people gathered to celebrate her father's life.

The community leader nodded and turned to receive a heaping plate of food. He passed it to Maliea and motioned for her to eat.

Reid was given an equally full plate of food and did his best to eat the offering.

A man at the edge of the circle produced a ukelele and played a song of lilting notes that sounded sad and sweet.

Women wearing matching blue dresses with crowns of green leaves danced into the center of the large circle, moving and swaying to the music.

The song ended. The women stopped dancing and waited for the next tune.

As the music started again, the ladies moved in

sync, swaying their hips and their arms gracefully moving in time to the ukelele.

Maliea leaned close to Reid. "They're telling a story of an island filled with happy people."

"Niihua?" Reid asked.

She nodded.

After more arm movements, Maliea's brow furrowed. "One dark night, a great storm swept over the island, bringing fierce winds, tearing roofs off homes. With the wind, a great boat slammed into the rocks on the windward side of the island."

"Redbeard's ship?" Reid asked.

Maliea shrugged and continued translating the movements. "The next morning, when the island people picked up the pieces of their homes, they spied the ship crushed against the rocks. They took their remaining canoes out to the ship.

"It had split in half. The people who'd been aboard had been swept away in the storm.

"Because their homes had been destroyed, they salvaged as much of the wood from the ship as they could get that day and carried it back to the village. They found gold, silver and precious stones in barrels lodged between the rocks. Having no need for such riches, they stashed the barrels in a cave and worked on rebuilding and reinforcing their homes with the planks taken from the broken ship."

Reid marveled at how the dancers' movements could tell so much of a story.

Maliea continued, "Another storm hit the island two nights later, sweeping what was left of the ship out to sea. The people of the village rebuilt their homes and resumed their happy lives, forgetting about the barrels in the cave."

Reid leaned close to Maliea's ear. "So, the treasure is or was here?"

Maliea nodded.

The song ended, and the women left the center of the circle. The ukelele player struck up another tune as people quietly talked among themselves.

The village elder spoke with Maliea for a long time.

Reid waited patiently for him to finish and Maliea to share what the man had said.

Maliea drew in a deep breath and nodded at something the elder said. She spoke and listened again. Finally, she turned to Reid, her expression grave.

"The villagers and the island owner, Elizabeth Sinclair, lived happily until opportunists came in search of the ship and the treasures it carried. The owner of the island, who'd sworn to protect the natives' heritage, refused to allow visitors on the island. Since the remainder of the ship had been swept away, there was no evidence it had run aground on the shores of Niihau."

"But that didn't stop the treasure hunters from looking, did it?" Reid said.

Maliea shook her head. "My father didn't come to the island following his clues. He came at the request of the current owners, Bruce and Keith Robinson, descendants of Elizabeth Sinclair. They had researched his work locating and preserving bits and pieces of Hawaiian heritage and culture. They knew he'd been interviewing descendants of the people who'd lived at the time of the great pirate raid. Because families passed down stories to their children, my father was able to piece together the ultimate location of the shipwreck."

"Were they worried he'd find it and bring a lot of attention to their island?" Reid asked.

Maliea shook her head. "No. The Robinsons are getting older and are tired of guarding the secret. They want the treasure moved from its current location to a museum, where it will be protected and shared with the people of Hawaii. They chose my father to make it happen. They trusted him to do it right and protect the folks of Niihau in the process."

Reid stared out at the people in the circle, eating, talking and laughing. "Moving the treasure would put an end to the constant worry of treasure hunters. The island people could live in peace."

"Exactly."

"What are they going to do now that your father's gone?" Reid asked. "Are they going to find someone else to manage the relocation?"

Maliea's twisted. "They want someone like my father who has the honesty, integrity and respect for the Hawaiian culture to manage the effort."

Reid's lips twitched and then spread into a wide grin. "Why not you?"

She snorted softly, pressing a hand to her chest. "I told him I couldn't do it alone. A treasure of such great value and the people who would work the relocation would need protection until it is safely placed in the hands of the chosen museum with appropriate security installed in its final resting place."

Reid frowned. "If word gets out before it makes it to a museum, it might turn into a media circus, bringing all kinds of crazies to Niihau."

"That's what the Robinsons are afraid of," Maliea said. "They want it handled on the down low. Once it's away from the island and at its final destination, they want the entire world to know the treasure has been found. Then, the people of Niihau can finally live in peace."

Reid met Maliea's gaze in the glow of the tiki torches. "You and the people enlisted to move the treasure will need protection."

She nodded. "I told him about a group of men who were loyal, honest and trustworthy. Men highly trained in combat who fought for our country and are now helping people in need of protection."

Reid reached for her hand and squeezed it gently. "The Brotherhood Protectors?"

She met his gaze. "Yes."

"It would be a huge honor to help these people. Hawk will agree wholeheartedly to support the effort. Hank Patterson as well."

"The elder will need to speak with the Robinsons," Maliea said. "He thinks they'll approve."

The community leader beside Maliea stood.

The music stopped, and people grew silent and rose to their feet.

Maliea and Reid pushed to their feet.

The elder spoke to the gathering, waving hands to the people and then to Maliea and Reid.

"He's thanking the people for the food and for coming together to celebrate the life of a good man, my father," Maliea said. "He's reminding them of how blessed they are to be a part of the Niihau community."

He spoke again and stepped backward, out of the circle, motioning for Maliea and Reid to follow.

Under the light of the millions of stars overhead, he walked through the village and up a slight hill to a large colonial house with wide porches and tall windows looking out to the sea.

He entered the house without using a key to unlock the door and led them up the stairs to a door along the upper landing. When he pushed it open, he said something to Maliea.

She nodded and spoke, then translated for Reid. "He's inviting us to stay in the owner's house and let me know the outhouse can be found out the back door several yards away."

The man held out his hand to Reid and spoke.

"He's thanking you for coming to his island, and if the owners are in agreement, he looks forward to working with you on the project to move the treasure."

Reid gripped the man's hand. "Tell him it's an honor, and I appreciate his trust in me and the Brotherhood Protectors. We will respect their people and their privacy. And thank him for their hospitality."

After Maliea relayed the message, the elder descended the stairs and left them alone in the owner's house.

Reid's groin tightened at the thought of sharing the night and the house with Maliea.

Maliea hesitated in front of the bedroom door. "I don't think he knows we aren't married. I'm sure it will be all right to use more than one bedroom."

Reid took her hands in his. "Is that what you want? For me to leave you alone? If it is, I will."

She stared up into his eyes in the dim light of the stars streaming through the far window. "I told you no strings."

"Do you want me to leave?" he asked again.

"Are we complicating this?" She took a step forward.

"If we do, is that a bad thing?" He raised her hands and pressed his lips to the backs of her knuckles.

"Maybe," she whispered.

"Do you want to kiss me?" he asked softly, pulling her into his arms. "Because I want to kiss you."

"Yes. Oh, yes." Maliea leaned up on her toes, her lips meeting his as he lowered his head to claim her mouth.

She opened to him immediately, her tongue tangling with his, her hands sliding up his chest to wrap around the back of his neck.

Reid had wanted to kiss her from when he'd woken that morning and throughout the day. Their one night together hadn't begun to quench his thirst for her. It had only made him want more.

When he raised his head, he stared down into her eyes. "What if I want strings?" he said without thinking.

She shook her head, her hands lowering to rest against his chest. "We barely know each other."

"We'll fix that by spending more time together on this project." He pressed a kiss to her forehead and then to each of her eyelids.

"I'm a package deal," she whispered.

"I know," he said with a smile. "Two for the

price of one. It's a hell of a deal. Nani is as amazing as her mother. Smart, kindhearted and beautiful."

"I'm so newly widowed," she argued. "You could be my rebound."

"He didn't do right by you and didn't deserve you or Nani." He kissed her cheek and then the tender area on her neck, just below her ear. "Got anything else?"

She laughed. "Give me a minute."

"Sweetheart, you have all night long." He held her gaze, all serious now. "Last chance to kick me out."

"Oh, what the hell," Maliea said. "You only live once."

He grinned down at her. "That's my girl."

"Stay. Make love with me." Maliea wrapped her arms around his neck and kissed him long and hard. "Tomorrow isn't guaranteed. I choose to live for today."

Reid's heart swelled, pushing out the hurt and betrayal that had tainted his thoughts on relationships since his divorce.

Maliea wasn't his ex-wife. She was so much more, and he suspected he'd only scratched the surface of how wonderful she was.

He swept her up in his arms and carried her into the bedroom, kicking the door shut behind them.

CHAPTER 14

DESPITE MAKING LOVE UNTIL MIDNIGHT, Maliea woke with the sun the following morning, feeling refreshed and happy. She opened her eyes to find Reid propped up on an elbow, staring down at her.

She smiled up at him. "Wow. I can't remember when I've ever slept better," she said, stretching an arm over her head. When she brought it down, she hooked it around the back of his neck and pulled him in for a kiss.

"Good morning to you, too," he said and pulled her naked body close to his. "Though I'd like to pick up where we left off last night, I hear movement downstairs. We might want to put on some clothes and see who's here beside us."

Maliea's eyes widened. "Yikes. They get up early around here." She pressed her body against his one last time, bumping up against his erection. "Mmm. Can I get a raincheck on this?"

"Absolutely." He kissed her again and then smacked her bare ass. "We'd better hustle before they come knocking on that door." He rolled out of the bed and onto his feet.

Maliea rolled out the other side of the bed, quickly dressed in her jeans and T-shirt and pulled on her shoes. Their hosts had brought their backpacks from the canoe and set them inside the door of the bedroom the day before. She rummaged in hers for her brush and quickly smoothed the tangles from her long hair.

All Reid had to do was run his hand through his hair, and it lay perfectly in place.

"Show-off," she said with a crooked grin as she eased the last tangle out.

"Ready?" he asked with his hand on the doorknob.

Maliea stowed her brush in her backpack and straightened. "Ready."

Reid held the door open for her and followed her out onto the landing.

They found the source of the noise in the house's kitchen. The appliances were antiques, dating back to a time when people still used wood-burning stoves to cook their·food.

A native Hawaiian woman with a long dark braid hanging down the middle of her back scooped fish from a skillet onto two plates and set them on the table next to cups of coconut milk.

She waved at the offering on the table.

"I guess this is breakfast," Maliea said and thanked the woman in her language.

Their cook smiled shyly and left them to eat, disappearing out the back door.

Reid held Maliea's chair as she took a seat at the table, looking around at the contents of the kitchen and the pictures on the wall. "This place could be straight out of the early nineteen hundreds."

"And still functional." Reid took a bite of the fish. "Not bad, although I don't remember the last time I had fish for breakfast."

Maliea smiled. "It is very good." She ate all the fish and washed it down with the coconut milk.

About the time they'd finished the meal, footsteps sounded on the front porch, hinges creaked and their host and guide from the night before appeared in the kitchen doorway. He wore what looked like shorts and nothing else, his dark-skinned chest bare, no shoes on his feet.

In Hawaiian, the man addressed Maliea. "You and your man will meet me at the dock." His gaze swept over her. "Wear what you can swim in."

She frowned. "Where are we going?"

"Meet me at the dock," he repeated, spun and left the kitchen.

Maliea's gaze followed the man until he disappeared down the hallway. The front door creaked and slammed shut.

She shifted her glance to Reid who looked to her for the translation. "I hope you brought swimwear. We're to meet him at the dock wearing something we can swim in."

Reid frowned. "That's it? No idea what he has in mind?"

Maliea's eyes narrowed and then widened. "Do you think he's going to take us to the treasure?"

"We'd better change and get down there before he has second thoughts," Reid said and headed for the stairs.

Maliea quickly stripped and slipped into her one-piece swimsuit, all the while trying not to be too obvious about staring at Reid's naked, tight ass.

The man had a sexy butt she'd love to spend more time running her hands over.

He pulled on his swim trunks and winked at her. "Caught you staring."

Her cheeks heated. "Can't help it. You have a really fine ass."

Reid pulled her into his arms. "Nothing compared to yours. Think they'd come looking for us if we didn't show up for another hour?"

Maliea wrapped her arms around his waist and sighed. "Sadly, yes." She looked up at him. "Let's get there and find out what this is all about."

Maliea slipped her shoes on, shoved the rest of her clothes into her backpack and slung it over her shoulder.

Reid did the same.

They left the house and headed for the dock, arriving to find their host and another man standing at the shore beside a canoe. The tide was further out than when they'd arrived the day before, forcing them to walk out to reach the water and the man with the canoe.

The elder motioned for Reid and Maliea to climb aboard.

Once they were in the canoe and seated, he pushed the canoe out into the water and stepped over the side, settling onto the front seat.

He and the man at the other end of the canoe lifted their paddles and dug into the water, sending the canoe skimming through the water.

For an older man, he was in good shape and didn't seem to struggle at all with the effort to propel the boat.

They followed the coastline for several minutes until they came to a point where waves crashed against the rocks just below the surface.

"The storm forced the pirate ship into the rocks here," the elder said, pointing to the jagged rocks.

Maliea relayed the information to Reid.

The men paddling the canoe swung wide of the

dangerous rocks and found a gap between giant slabs. Timing with the waves, they waited a moment and then sent the canoe through to a calmer pool on the other side and in front of what appeared to be a sheer rock cliff.

They ran the canoe up against a flat table rock a foot above the water's edge.

The elder stepped out of the canoe and held out a hand to Maliea.

She took the hand and scrambled out of the canoe onto the rock ledge.

Reid stepped out of the canoe beside her.

Between the two Hawaiian men, they dragged the canoe up onto the rock ledge and secured it with a knotted line wedged into a crevice.

The elder pointed to the rock cliff. "We swim," he said in his language and motioned with his hand, indicating they would go beneath the surface and come back up.

Maliea stared at the rock cliff, her pulse kicking into high gear. "Is the cave entrance underwater?" she asked.

The elder nodded.

"What's he saying," Reid asked.

Maliea told him.

"I'm not sure I like this," Reid said. "How good are you at swimming and holding your breath?"

She stared at the dark water. "I learned to swim

as a baby. Because we live on an island, my mother and father insisted I be a competent swimmer. I also learned to surf. But I've been so busy trying to make a living, I haven't been in the water for a while."

"Then stay here," Reid said. "I'll go with them and check it out."

Maliea shook her head. "No. It's okay. If our guide can do this, I should be fine." She nodded toward the elder and told him she was ready.

His partner slipped into the water, took a deep breath and dove beneath the surface.

Maliea watched his body move through the water until it disappeared.

The elder pointed to Maliea and then back at himself, indicating she should go with him.

Maliea nodded, shared a glance with Reid and slipped into the water beside the elder.

As he drew in a breath, so did Maliea.

Then he ducked beneath the surface.

Maliea did the same, swimming hard, determined to remain abreast of him and hoping Reid was right behind them.

The elder came to a place where the water was bluer, almost iridescent, lighting their way through an opening in the rock wall. Here, the seafloor was sandy, reflecting sunlight from somewhere.

Just when Maliea's lungs started to burn with

the need to take another breath, the elder pushed up from the sandy sea floor.

Maliea followed him and broke through the surface into a cave with sunlight streaming in from a hole directly overhead. She sucked in a full lungful of air and tread water.

Reid popped up beside her. No sooner had he taken a breath when he asked her, "Are you all right?"

She nodded. "It wasn't bad. Not knowing how far you have to go was the worst part. Now that I know, I won't be as freaked out on the way back through."

"Same," Reid said and looked around the interior of the cave.

The elder and his partner had climbed up on a rocky ledge several feet above the water.

The elder waited until he had Maliea's attention and then pointed to a ledge above the highest waterline.

Maliea swam over to the ledge where the elder stood and pulled herself up to sit on the rock.

Reid climbed up beside her and stood. He helped her to her feet and fell in behind her as she followed the elder and his buddy to the upper ledge.

The upper level went further back into the cave than Maliea had expected, giving them plenty of room to move about without having to bend over.

As her eyes adjusted to the darker recesses, Maliea could make out several wooden barrels lined up against the wall.

The elder stood beside one with a fishing knife in his hand. He dug the tip of the knife into the barrel's wooden top and worked it free.

When he lifted the lid, Maliea peered into the shadowy interior.

She didn't need a flashlight to see the shiny gold coins filling the barrel's interior.

Maliea backed away and let Reid see what was inside.

When he turned to meet her gaze, he said. "We need to get Hawk and the entire team out here ASAP. There's enough gold in there to kill for."

"Only if they know where to find it," Maliea said. "The people of Niihua have hidden this secret for over a century."

"We need to get this stuff moved."

"That's why we're here," Maliea assured him. "They wanted us to assess our needs, to know what has to be moved."

"I have my satellite phone in my backpack," Reid turned toward the ledge. "Come on. Let's get out of here so I can call in backup."

Maliea followed him. "Are you that worried?"

He dropped over the side to the level below and held out his arms to assist her in her descent. "I have a bad feeling about this."

"What's the worst that could happen?" she said. "Someone comes in and steals it?"

He helped her down to the ledge where he stood and stared down in her eyes. "The worst thing that could happen?" He shook his head. "Someone kills these gentle people to take all this gold." His voice lowered, his gaze intense. "Someone hurts you to get to this." He turned and descended from the ledge into the water below. "I wish they hadn't brought us here until we had a full contingent of protectors as backup."

Maliea had never seen Reid so wound up and actually scared. She slipped into the water beside him. "I don't understand why you're so upset."

"Don't you see?" He waved a hand toward the upper level. "You've seen the treasure. You know where it is. The people who've been following you already think you're on the right track. If they think you can lead them to it, they might not hesitate to hurt you or Nani to get you to bring them here." He cupped her cheeks in his hands. "You're not safe as long as this treasure is here. We have to get to that satellite phone and get Hawk and the rest of the team out here as soon as possible."

Maliea's heartbeat raced, pounding against her chest. Would the people who'd been following her, destroying her home and her father's, use a child as leverage to get her to bring them to the treasure?

"Let's get to that satellite phone," she said. "I

need to hear my daughter's voice. I need to know she's safe." Maliea dove into the water and swam for the cave entrance, desperate to get out and call Hawk and Kalea. She hoped Reid was wrong and had spooked her for nothing. Until she heard Nani's sweet voice, she couldn't think straight.

Reid swam beside her. When they reached the cave entrance, he went through first. For a moment, she couldn't see him, which made her even more unnerved.

The sooner she got out of the cave, the sooner she could breathe.

As REID EMERGED from the cave entrance, something long and thin shot through the water, narrowly missing his head.

It wasn't until he spotted a man in scuba gear swimming toward him with a spear gun that he realized the long, narrow projectile had been a deadly spear.

His immediate thought went to Maliea, who would be coming out of the cave behind him. If he swam back to her, the man who'd just fired a spear gun at him would follow him to Maliea.

Reid swam straight for the guy, determined to disarm and neutralize him before he could hurt Maliea.

The diver dropped the spear gun, pulled a

wicked dive knife from a sheath attached to his wrist and came at Reid.

Without breathing apparatus or a weapon to defend himself, Reid was at a distinct disadvantage. He didn't let that slow him down. His training as a Navy SEAL kicked in, giving him laser focus on his opponent. As he neared, he waited until the last possible second to reach for the attacker's outstretched hand, wielding the knife.

The water slowed his movement, but it also slowed the other guy's.

Reid missed grabbing the man's wrist as he swung the knife at Reid's chest.

The tip of the blade narrowly missed its mark. On the man's return swipe, Reid caught his wrist and deflected the second jab from grazing his arm.

The diver jerked his hand free and came at Reid again. By that time, Reid's lungs burned. He had to surface for air soon, or it would all be over. Ready to end the nonsense, he kicked hard, swimming straight into the man's blade. He grabbed the diver's hand in a death grip, yanked it upward and back behind the man's head. In a quick, decisive move, Reid hooked the blade around the regulator hose, slicing into the thick rubber.

Bubbles erupted from the damaged hose.

The diver spit the regulator from his mouth and immediately headed for the surface.

Reid followed, catching up with him as the man

neared the surface. He grabbed his fin and pulled him back before his head cleared the water.

He kicked, trying to shake Reid loose, but Reid snagged the other fin and pulled him deeper.

With the knife still clutched in his hand, the diver swiped at Reid, his movements growing more desperate with each passing second. When he couldn't shake Reid loose, he released his hold on the knife and used his arms in an attempt to swim to the surface, dragging Reid with him.

Reid held on, not making it any easier for the man, yet needing to surface just as badly.

At the last minute, he pulled the man down, stepped onto his tank and pushed himself to the surface.

He'd barely sucked in a breath when a hand grabbed his ankle and dragged him back under.

With no weapon to end it quickly and no way to get his arm around the man's neck with the scuba tank in the way, Reid's only recourse was to get in front of the man and use his fists to subdue him.

In the back of Reid's mind, he knew that with each passing second it took him to neutralize the diver, Maliea remained unprotected. What worried him even more was that she had yet to reach the surface.

Channeling every ounce of strength and determination, he attacked his opponent, slamming his fist into the man's face.

At first, he blocked some of the punches. As the diver weakened, Reid landed more hits, finally knocking the man out.

Without wasting another moment, he took a deep breath and went back for Maliea, praying he wasn't too late.

CHAPTER 15

JUST AS MALIEA reached the cave entrance and started to swim through, she saw a razor-sharp spear zip past Reid's head and bounce against the rock face of the cliff above the cave's opening.

Reid swam straight at the man, who pulled a knife out and swung it at Reid.

Maliea started toward Reid to help him overcome his attacker, but something gripped her ankle and yanked her back.

Maliea turned to find another diver holding on tightly to her ankle, dragging her deeper.

She kicked at the hand on her ankle, and though the hand was small, its grip was relentless. The diver refused to let go.

When long yellow strands floated out behind the diver's head, Maliea realized the diver was female. And she wasn't going to let Maliea reach the surface without a fight.

If she wanted a fight, she was going to get one. Maliea had to free herself to help Reid, and this bitch had to go.

Instead of struggling to get to the surface, Maliea turned on her captor. The first thing she could get her hands on was the woman's hair. She twisted her fingers into the long blond strands and pulled as hard as she could.

As soon as the hand on her ankle released its hold, Maliea grabbed the next thing she could reach—the regulator hose.

Planting her feet against the woman's chest, she yanked on the hose, pulling it free of the female's mouth.

Desperate for air, Maliea quickly shoved the regulator into her own mouth and pulled in a little bit of air before something sharp sliced into her side.

She twisted, kicking hard to get away.

The woman stuck the mouthpiece of the regulator back in her mouth and came at Maliea again with the knife in her hand.

With adrenaline pumping through her veins, Maliea didn't slow down enough to feel pain. She had no choice but to stop this bitch. If she succeeded in killing Maliea, she'd go after Reid and help her partner take him out.

Maliea couldn't let her do that. She had a child waiting for her to return and a relationship to fully explore with a former Navy SEAL who'd made her feel more alive than she had in a long time.

Maliea summoned her inner warrior and met the woman head-on. As the diver swung the knife, Maliea dodged the tip and snagged her wrist. She twisted it sharply, aiming the point in the opposite direction at the same time as she grabbed the BCD and pulled sharply toward her, slamming her body into her own hand and gripping the woman's hand with the knife.

The woman's eyes widened in the face mask. Her body went limp as a cloud of red drifted upward.

Starving for air, Maliea kicked hard, heading for the surface. Though the woman had tried to kill her, Maliea couldn't leave her to die. She dragged her with her every stroke of the way.

Just when she thought she wouldn't make it, Reid appeared beside her.

The elder came up on her other side and relieved her of her burden, taking the female driver the rest of the way to the surface.

Her lack of oxygen made her vision blur as a gray haze threatened to consume her. Reid swam harder, pulling her up with him. On the verge of blacking out, Maliea exploded out of the water. Holding onto Reid, she sucked air into her lungs, breathing in and out several times before her vision cleared and the gray fog dissipated.

A thumping sound grew louder as the bright orange fuselage of a US Coast Guard helicopter swooped in and hovered over their position.

Reid trod water, holding onto Maliea as a cable lowered a man into the water beside Reid and Maliea.

"Take her first," Reid said and started to hand her over into the care of the Coast Guard rescue swimmer.

Maliea shook her head. "No. Want to stay with you."

Reid kissed her forehead. "You're injured. I'm not. You have to let them help you. Don't worry, I'll catch up with you later. Someone has to secure this site."

Moments later, they hoisted her and the rescue swimmer up into the helicopter. She didn't want to leave Reid down there in the water. What if another bad guy came after him? She tried to sit up but a hand on her shoulder kept her from moving.

She stared up in Jace Hawkin's eyes and blinked. "How..." she forced air past her vocal cords, "...did you know to come?"

"Swede had set up an alert on Mark Laster's credit card. When he saw that Mark Laster had turned in the rental car at the airport, caught a flight to Kauai and rented a jet boat, we figured you might be in trouble. The man's prints on the car matched those in the apartments. We tracked the satellite phone I gave him to find you. Kalea and Mr. Parker put in a distress call to the US Coast Guard. They picked me up on the way across the Big Island. Seems we made it just in time."

"Thank you," Maliea laid back, all energy drained from her body. "Nani?" she asked.

"Your daughter and Kalea are bonding over a litter of puppies they found in the barn. She's fine and happy."

Maliea smiled, fighting hard but succumbing to the darkness that dragged her under.

She drifted in and out of consciousness throughout the flight. Each time she came to, she asked for Reid and Nani. Each time, she blacked out again.

The next time she surfaced, she opened her eyes to bright lights shining down from the ceiling of a hospital room. One arm had an IV in it, and her other arm was weighed down by a hand holding hers.

Maliea turned to find Reid's handsome face smiling back at her. "How did you get here so fast," she asked, her words coming out in a series of croaks.

He lifted her hand to his lips. "I'm quick like that. And you've been asleep for over twenty-four hours."

She frowned. "I must have been really tired."

He shook his head. "You had surgery. The knife wound resulted in some internal bleeding. They went in laparoscopically and plugged the holes. Thankfully, none of your important organs were damaged. They'll probably let you leave later today."

"Nani?" she asked.

"Is still on the Big Island with Mr. Parkman and Kalea. She misses you but has discovered a new love of horseback riding." He chuckled. "She wants you to buy her a pony."

"Not only can I not afford to purchase a pony, but I also can't afford to keep it," Maliea closed her eyes and pinched the bridge of her nose. "Could you break the news to her? I can't."

"You don't have to. Hawk and Kalea offered to let you and Nani stay with them whenever you like. Nani can ride her favorite pony every time."

"They don't understand," Maliea said, refusing to open her eyes to the glare of the overhead light. "I can't fly us out to visit every month when I can barely afford to pay rent."

"You know, you wouldn't have to worry about paying rent if you got a roommate."

"My friends all have roommates."

"Hey," Reid said. "Look at me."

Maliea turned toward him and opened her eyes.

"I'm trying to tell you I need a roommate," Reid

said. "My work takes me away often, and I need someone to water my plants and look after my dog."

"You have a dog?" Maliea frowned. "You never said you had a dog. Nani's been asking for one since she turned two. I keep telling her it's too hard to keep a dog while living in an apartment."

He cupped her cheek, then met and held her gaze. "Focus, woman."

Her brow wrinkled. "What kind of dog do you have?" she asked.

He laughed. "Whatever kind of dog you and Nani want. I'm trying to ask you and Nani to come live with me."

Her frown deepened. "Where?"

"I don't know. We'll find a house with a yard so Nani can have a dog and a sister when Abby comes to visit."

Hope swelled in her chest before she could remind herself they didn't know each other very well. "Are you serious?"

"As serious as sin."

"We don't know each other. I didn't even know you had a dog."

His lips twitched. "I don't. I think you're still loopy from anesthesia."

"I think you're loopy from lack of oxygen. How long were you underwater fighting that man?"

"Long enough."

"Was he that Mark Laster guy who was listening outside the cabin?"

Reid nodded.

"Who was the woman?" Maliea's eyes widened. "Did she live? Please tell me she did. I've never killed someone before."

"She lived, and she's your favorite Teacher's Assistant."

"That was Heather?" Maliea's head spun. "I was willing to forgive her for taking my husband. He wasn't the right one for me. But she's turning out to be a major pain in my side." A twinge of pain made her wince. "Was she using Taylor and my father to find the treasure?"

Reid nodded. "Swede traced the payment to Laster to an account in the Cayman Islands. After digging deeper through the maze of corporations associated with the account, he came up with an owner, Jonathan Walters, a ruthless businessman known for hostile takeovers and his slash-and-burn policy of buying companies, then stripping them down to the bone and selling them."

"Heather's last name is Walters," Maliea said. "Are they related?"

"Heather is his daughter. When he threatened to cut her off for wrecking her third car in as many months while attending grad school, she decided to make her own fortune in treasure hunting."

"Not so easy money, is it bitch?" Maliea murmured, resting a hand on her sore belly.

Reid frowned. "Are you hurting? Do you need some pain medication?"

Maliea sighed. "No. I need to know someone is looking after the treasure. I feel responsible for it."

"Hank Patterson is calling in the big guns to move it. The Robinsons are happy to bring them on for protection services, and they want you to coordinate with the Bishop Museum to house the exhibit. Hank and his wife Sadie will fund the upgrade in the security system they'll need to protect the lost treasure of Red Beard."

"Who'd guarding it now?" she asked.

"Members of the Brotherhood Protectors. They're scheduled to load and move it next week."

"Which means I need to get out of bed and get to work."

"Oh, and the State of Hawaii is granting you a full ride to the University of Hawaii for your undergraduate degree through your doctorate, honoring your father and his work to preserve the Hawaiian culture."

Maliea sat up and winced, falling back against the mattress. "Are you kidding me? Because, if you are, it's not funny."

Reid held up his hand. "SEALs honor. It is conditional on your studies including the preservation of the Hawaiian culture."

"Done." A grin spread across her face. "My father would've been so proud to know I carried on his work."

"Your daughter will be proud of her mother." He raised his eyebrows. "Now, back to the question of roommates..."

Her smile slipped. "Shouldn't we get to know each other before we take such a big step? I have a daughter to think of and set the example for."

"Fair enough. If you need more time to get to know me and fall in love, I'll give you all the time you need. You and Nani can each have your own room in our house. We can date for a set number of weeks, abstain from having sex during that time and then discuss resuming sex at that point."

Maliea frowned.

"Not enough time?" Reid asked. "We can date longer."

"Can we negotiate the part about abstinence?" she asked. "A shorter timeframe, not longer. Are you sure you want this? Moving in together is so permanent. Are you sure you'll want me to stay?"

"Maliea," Reid said. "I'd ask you to marry me today if I thought you'd agree."

"You would?" she asked. "Why?"

A crooked smile spread across his face. He lifted a shoulder and let it fall. "I never thought I'd say this until I met you, but when you know, you know."

Maliea's heart nearly burst with the flood of happiness spreading through her. "Come here."

He leaned closer.

"No," she said and patted the bed. "Come here."

His brow furrowed. "You just had surgery."

She scooted over, wincing with the twinges of pain. This time, she pointed to the empty space she'd made beside her. "Here. Now."

Reid chuckled and eased up onto the bed beside her.

"I don't need weeks to get to know you. I just wanted you to have the time to get to know me and Nani. She's a three-year-old. She's not a perfect angel every day of the week. Teen years are supposed to be the worst, and I don't want to drag her in and out of relationships."

"She's already got me wrapped around her little finger. I'll love that kid as much as I already love her mother." He brushed a strand of Maliea's hair back behind her ear. "I know you're a package deal, and I'm all in. I already know your heart is big enough to love my Abby as well. The girls will love having a sister and would welcome more siblings." His eyes widened. "Do you want more children? Because if you don't, we already have two perfect girls."

Maliea pressed a finger to his lips. "Yes. I want more children. I always wanted a houseful of little voices and giggles."

"Let's give it a go," Reid said. "If we feel the same in a month, we can make it official."

"You'll make a proper proposal?" she asked.

"Down on one knee, flowers, a ring—the whole shebang."

"You know what?" Maliea said. "I don't need a month. I don't need a week without sex. I don't need a proper proposal. What I need is you. Reid Johnson, I'm falling more deeply in love with you every day, every hour and every minute I spend with you."

"Are you sure?" he asked.

"Honey, when you know...you know." Maliea pulled him close. "And I really want to kiss you."

EPILOGUE

Four years later

REID LEANED his elbows on the fence rail at the Parkman Ranch. Maliea stood beside him, smiling at Kalea and Hawk, leading a horse around the corral with their three-year-old daughter sitting in the saddle, her legs too short to reach the stirrups, a happy grin wreathing her face.

"Reminds me of when Nani went for her first ride, with Kalea and Hawk patiently leading her around."

The sound of horse hooves pounded the ground, racing toward the barn.

"Here come the girls," Reid said.

Nani, on her favorite gelding, and Abby, on her

mare, flew toward them, their hair flying out behind them—Nani, so exotically dark, and Abby, golden-haired and light. They'd loved each other immediately and had become pen pals, as well as exchanging social media handles and phone numbers.

At Abby's insistence, her mother let her spend more weeks in Hawaii during the summer where she and Nani were learning to ride horses, swim and surf.

The girls dismounted and led their horses into the barn. They came out a few minutes after brushing and feeding their mounts.

"Where are you going now?" Maliea asked.

Nani stopped in front of her mother. "We're going to swim in the pool."

Abby came to stand beside her. "After we swim, we're having a spa day, painting our fingernails and curling our hair."

"Later, Mom," Nani said, bent and kissed Maliea's swollen belly. "Hello, little brother. Hurry up and come out to play." She skipped away, heading for the house.

Abby bent and kissed Maliea's belly. "Don't listen to Nani, little sister. We know you're a girl. I can't wait to introduce you to celestial blue nail polish. Can't wait to meet you."

Abby skipped away after Nani.

Maliea rubbed her belly. "I'm glad I was able to finish my undergrad and master's before the baby arrives. I don't know if I can juggle full-time school and a newborn, along with the two very active seven-year-olds."

"Oh, that reminds me," Reid said. "Your box of books arrived today."

Maliea clapped her hands, smiling. "I was hoping they'd get here before the baby. I think my father would have loved that I finished his story-book and published it. The Bishop Museum requested two cases of them to sell in the gift shop."

"I opened the box," Reid admitted. "They looked amazing."

"I'm so glad," Maliea said. "They should earn money for the museum."

"On a somber note..." Reid rested a hand against the small of her back, "I heard Heather Walters is out on parole."

Maliea's eyes widened. "Should I be concerned?"

"I don't think so," Reid said. "She found religion while incarcerated. Her father funded the construction of a church for her, and she's booking speaking engagements across the country."

Maliea smiled. "I'm glad for her. I couldn't hold a grudge. It takes too much of my time and energy when I have much better things to do."

Reid grinned. "Like kissing?"

She turned to him. "Do you want to kiss me, Reid Johnson?" Her hand rested on his chest as she lowered her voice to the sexy tone he really loved to hear. "Because I really want to kiss you."

EMI'S HERO

BROTHERHOOD PROTECTORS HAWAII
BOOK #5

New York Times & *USA Today*
Bestselling Author

ELLE JAMES

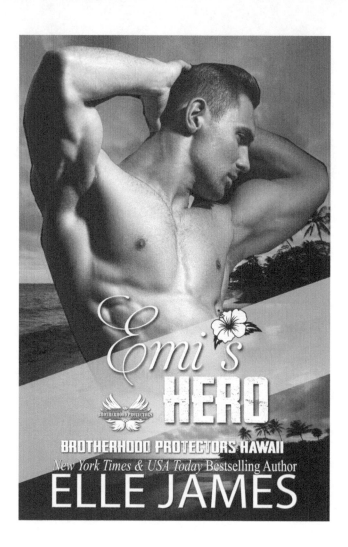

Emi's

HERO

BROTHERHOOD PROTECTORS HAWAII

New York Times & *USA Today* Bestselling Author

ELLE JAMES

CHAPTER 1

"WHY AREN'T you wearing the swimsuit I told you to wear?" Fallon Vance stalked out onto the deck of the yacht, his dark eyebrows dipped low on his forehead. "I wanted to see you in the red one, not this..." his nostrils flared, and his lips curled back in a sneer, "boring black, one-piece abomination. I don't keep you for boring."

Emi Sands lifted her chin. He shouldn't keep her at all. "The strap broke," she said, hiding the truth behind a poker face she'd perfected over the years. She'd deliberately ripped the strap off the bra of the suit. She wanted to tell him that she hated it, that the suit displayed more than it covered. She didn't like wearing it, especially around her young daughter.

But she couldn't say anything that might direct

attention to her daughter. Her sweet Sara was the only thing keeping her there. The only reason she hadn't tried to escape.

Escape.

She'd dreamed of escape for the first four years he'd held her captive. She'd tried on a number of occasions, only to be heavily sedated and kept on mind-numbing drugs until she'd gotten pregnant with Sara.

Since then, he'd used the baby growing inside her, and then the child she'd given birth to, as leverage to keep her compliant.

He hadn't needed the drugs anymore. Sure, she might eventually find a way to leave the bastard, but leaving with a small child...

Impossible.

And she wouldn't leave without Sara.

She remained stuck with a horrible, abusive monster who kept her like a dog on a chain, threatening her every time she dared to suggest he let her and Sara leave.

He kept her locked away on his compound with its high walls topped with concertina wire. His employees were either foreigners who barely spoke English and were probably part of the human trafficking chain, or highly paid mercenaries who would do anything he asked of them—including kill.

Fallon had insisted on her accompanying him

on his yacht for a few days away from the compound, fishing and boating around the islands. Thankfully, he'd agreed to let Sara remain behind with Maria, one of the cleaning staff from Guatemala. Though she barely spoke English, she was Emi's only friend in the compound.

Emi didn't want to go anywhere with Fallon, especially not on his yacht. Most often, he liked to take the helm and drive like a maniac, much faster than prudent.

The poor captain would stand back with his fists clenched around a rail, holding tightly and praying his boss didn't flip the boat and send them all to the bottom of the ocean.

Emi almost wished Fallon would flip the boat and put them all out of their misery. But then, what would happen to little Sara? Perhaps someone would find her and place her in foster care. Maybe there, she'd be happier and learn not to be afraid of all men.

"Fix the suit and put it on," Fallon spat. He didn't release his hold on the swimsuit.

"I don't have a needle and thread," Emi pointed out.

"Then tie the damned thing," Fallon shouted and turned the wheel sharply, causing the ship to lean sharply on the port side.

Emi staggered across the deck and slammed

into the shiny metal railing. Pain shot through her hip.

"Go, bitch," Fallon called out. "You have exactly two minutes to get it right."

The "or else" didn't need to be stated.

Emi knew it was implied. If she didn't show up on the deck in two minutes, he'd beat her like he'd done so many times over the past eight years.

She hurried down the steps into the stateroom below, grabbed the top of the red suit with the torn strap and tied it together with shaking fingers. As soon as it held together, she stripped out of the one-piece and fit the bra over her breasts.

One minute had passed.

Emi jammed her legs into the thong bikini and pulled it up over her thighs. Without checking her reflection, she raced back up the steps onto the deck, approaching the helm at two and a half minutes, hoping Fallon hadn't noticed she'd taken longer than he'd given.

Fallon stood tall behind the helm, staring out at the ocean in front of him. With smooth deliberation, he raised his hand and glanced down at the Rolex watch on his wrist. "Two minutes and forty-six seconds," he said, his tone cold and biting. "How long did I give you?"

Emi swallowed hard on the fear closing her throat and answered, "Two minutes."

"Captain!" Fallon called out and released his hold on the wheel.

The yacht's captain stepped forward and took the helm, averting his gaze from Emi. None of Fallon's staff members questioned the boss. To do so could cost their jobs.

They also understood that their jobs weren't all it could cost them. Some of the people who had displeased Fallon the most had disappeared. Emi suspected they hadn't made it past the wall of the compound.

Fallon didn't let go of what he considered his property. If he did allow a staff member to leave, that person could spread the word that he was holding people hostage on his estate.

Like he'd held her hostage since he'd stolen her away from her college friends that fateful day eight years ago.

Emi wondered if her folks had given up on her. When they'd been informed of their daughter's disappearance, had they flown out to Hawaii to help find her?

They hadn't had a lot of money. Emi had worked part-time while going to college and full-time in the summers. Some of her friends' parents had a more secure financial situation and could afford to send their daughters to Hawaii on Spring Break. Emi had earned the money she'd needed to pay for her flight and her portion of the room and rental car.

Emi had worked at the diner up to the last minute before she had turned in her apron and rushed out the door to catch her flight. She'd been too tired to party their first night in Hawaii. The flight had been long, and her friends had talked all the way, excited and ready to make the best of their last spring break before graduation.

She hadn't been in Honolulu but a few hours when she'd left her group of friends at a bar to walk back to the hotel. So often since that night, she'd wished she'd stayed with her friends, no matter how tired she'd been.

Second-guessing her choice did nothing to improve her situation. She had to do whatever it took to survive and protect Sara.

Fallon gripped Emi's arm and marched her through the yacht, his fingers digging into her flesh. She'd have bruises to add to the collection across her body.

He rarely hit her face, not that it mattered. She never came into contact with anyone who didn't work for Fallon. His employees didn't stick up for her when Fallon beat her. Some of them had bruises much like hers.

The man had a violent temper, and even the smallest infractions set him off.

Forty-six seconds and a red bikini would be his latest trigger.

Emi had learned not to fight back. It only made him more violent. The only time she'd fought back, Fallon had almost killed her. He'd left her on the floor to die, refusing to take her to a hospital.

Emi had wished she was dead. But her heart had kept beating, she'd still breathed, and her wounds and broken ribs had healed.

Out of the corner of her eye, she could see the telltale flush of ruddy red staining Fallon's neck and cheeks. Her heart plummeted into her belly.

He was mad. Really mad.

Why had she dressed in the one-piece? What had possessed her to rip the strap off the red bikini top?

He brought her to the back deck and slung her around like a ragdoll. "When I tell you to do something, I expect it to be done. Every order must be carried out precisely."

Emi bowed her head, refusing to look into his eyes, at the hatred and maniacal gleam that always preceded a beating. "I'm sorry. It won't happen again," she murmured.

"But it does. Again and again," he said his voice low and dangerous. "What's it going to take to make you compliant?"

"I promise," she said. "It won't happen again."

"You're insolent, disrespectful and you spend

too much time with that brat of yours. I should never have let you keep it."

It?

Fallon didn't even consider Sara a human. She was a beautiful child. He was the biological father. The man was anything but a father to his own little girl. He scared her.

Although Sara was only three, she'd come to Emi's defense on more than one occasion when Fallon had tried to hurt her.

Emi had been afraid the monster would hurt Sara for trying to help her mother. She did her best to keep her daughter away from Fallon.

It.

Emi shook her head slowly, counting to ten to keep from saying her daughter was more of a human than Fallon ever would be. He was a sperm donor. Nothing more.

"Yeah. You're too involved with the kid. I should've had them carry the kid out with the bloody sheets. I still think I might do it."

Despite her determination to maintain a poker face, Emi's head jerked up, her eyes widening. "She's a child. Not an *it*," she said, her voice low and fierce. "She's done nothing to hurt you."

His eyes narrowed. "You've become more insolent and disobedient since I allowed you to have her."

"I forgot myself," she said, trying to tamp down her anger and fear, knowing it wouldn't help the situation with Fallon. "Trust me, I won't do it again."

He snorted. "I don't trust you. You're a useless woman when you aren't obeying my orders. And I have no use for children. They're a distraction. I don't know why I let you keep her. I think it's time to remove her from the property."

All the pent-up emotions she'd held back for years exploded inside Emi. "No!" She raised her fists and pounded them against his chest. "She's my child. You can't take her away."

Fallon snagged her wrists in a tight grip, yanked her close and sneered into her face. "I can do whatever the hell I want," he said, his voice low and dangerous. "I own you. I own your brat. I own the people who work for me. No one cares about you or that little shit. The only reason you're alive today is because I allow you to live. Remember that. And if I say the brat has to go, it goes." He shoved her away from him, releasing her wrists. "Hit me again, and you'll pay."

"Anyone who could throw a child away like so much garbage is a monster," she said between gritted teeth. She should have stopped there, but she couldn't, the words pouring out unguarded. "You can't get a woman to sleep with you, so you hold us prisoner so you can rape us whenever you like. You're a bastard, a colossal asshole and your dick is as small and insignificant as your mind."

Fallon's narrowed eyes became ominous slits.

He crossed his right arm over his chest and then swung it out, backhanding her so hard that her head snapped to the right, and she flew across the deck. Her hip hit the rail so hard, she tipped over the shiny metal rail. She reached out in an attempt to grab for it. Her fingers only grasped air as her momentum carried her body over the side of the yacht.

With her head spinning and pain making her world grow dark, she fell. As if in slow motion, she plunged into the water below, sinking beneath the surface, churned by the yacht's wake.

The abrupt dunking triggered survival mode in her hazy mind. She kicked her feet, unsure of which direction was up. Her body churned in the water thrust out by the propellers. The knot she'd tied on her swimsuit top must have come loose in her fall. The red bikini top lost in the sea was the least of her worries.

When she'd fallen overboard, she hadn't had time to catch a breath. If she didn't surface quickly, she'd drown.

Her first clear thought was of Sara. If Emi died, what would happen to her daughter?

Panic pushed back the threatening darkness.

The more Emi flailed in the water, the more

disoriented she became. Her chest burned with the need to breathe.

She remembered what she'd read before she'd come to Hawaii, something about snorkeling and scuba. *Watch which way the bubbles go. They always rise to the surface.*

Emi forced herself to be still and let out the last little bit of air still in her lungs.

For what seemed an eternity of the second it took for the bubble to orient, she watched. As soon as the bubble established a direction, Emi kicked her feet, chasing the bubble all the way to the surface.

As her head breached, she sucked in air, filling her lungs.

She looked ahead at the vast expanse of ocean.

Where was the yacht?

Her heart still thundering against her ribs, she spun in the water, waves splashing up into her face.

A small spec on the water's surface grew even smaller. With no other shape on the water besides small waves, that had to be the yacht.

Fear and despair washed over her like a tsunami.

"Wait!" she cried and waved her arm.

The spec on the water didn't slow or turn around. It disappeared into the distance, leaving Emi alone in the ocean with no other vessel in sight, no land to swim toward and no hope.

Tears joined the water splashing against her cheeks.

"No," she moaned. "He'll kill her. He'll kill Sara."

Emi couldn't let this be the end of her. She had to make her way back to land, find help and get to Sara before Fallon. She prayed Maria would find a way to hide her little girl, at least until Emi found a way back to save her.

Striking out in the opposite direction from where the yacht had disappeared, Emi swam, pacing herself for what could be a long way back to shore, fighting back the gloom and doom of the what-ifs.

What if she wasn't going in the right direction? What if she never made it back to shore? What if some sea creature decided she looked like a tasty snack? What if she was out there for days without food and water?

Determined not to succumb to negativity, she focused on the positive.

The saltwater made it easier for her to stay afloat. Since it was still considered summer, the water temperature was relatively warm, though still lower than her own core temperature. The longer she was in the water, the colder she would get.

She had to keep moving. Not only to find land but to keep from getting hypothermia.

Minutes passed, the sun beating down on her,

keeping her warm. The sunscreen she'd applied earlier probably had been washed away in the tumbling effect of the water spun up by the yacht's propellers.

She couldn't let that worry her as she alternated strokes between freestyle and breaststroke. When the muscles in her arms began to cramp with the effort, she flipped onto her back to rest and float, kicking her feet to keep moving.

The sun slowly sank toward the horizon, sparing her burning skin but taking the warmth with it. As darkness settled over the ocean, despair filled her chest. How could she keep moving through the night when exhaustion crept into every muscle, nerve and cell?

Sara.

She couldn't give up. Dying would be the easy way out for Emi. But Sara had an entire life ahead of her. If she got to her soon enough. That beautiful little girl deserved a life. One filled with happiness and joy. Not the existence she'd been forced to live in from the day she'd been born.

Sara deserved to live.

Her daughter's name became the mantra pushing her forward when she thought she had no strength left.

Sara. Sara. Sara.

Emi kept moving.

I can do this. I can make it another hour.

Stars blinked to life in the heavens above, lighting her way.

The sea calmed, making it easier for her to push on.

Another hour. I can do this. For Sara.

The night seemed to last forever.

Please. Please. Please let the morning sun rise. I'll take a break. I'll float. I'll regain my strength.

She couldn't stop in the dark. Her body was losing heat even as she moved. If she stopped, she might succumb to the cold.

Her daughter's image swam into her mind. Her strawberry blond hair curling around her cheeks, her beautiful green eyes a mirror of her own looking into Emi's soul, urging her to come back.

I'm coming, baby.

Sara. Sara. Sara.

When she thought she couldn't lift her arms one more stroke or kick her legs one more time, the gray light of dawn lightened the horizon, giving her a direction to aim for. They'd left the island the previous morning with the sun at their backs, heading west. Surely, she would see land soon.

Her arms and legs hurt so much she had to flip onto her back and float.

Just for a minute or two.

Beyond tired, she could do nothing else. She closed her eyes and breathed in and out. The gentle rocking motion felt good. Too good.

Emi drifted off, waking with a start when water washed over her face.

"Can't sleep," she said, her voice nothing more than a whisper carried away on the ocean breeze.

Her eyes closed again.

Exhaustion claimed her.

Thank you for reading Maliea's Hero and the first chapter of Emi's Hero.
If you want to read more about Emi's Hero
click Here

ABOUT THE AUTHOR

ELLE JAMES also writing as MYLA JACKSON is a *New York Times* and *USA Today* Bestselling author of books including cowboys, intrigues and paranormal adventures that keep her readers on the edges of their seats. When she's not at her computer, she's traveling, snow skiing, boating, or riding her ATV, dreaming up new stories. Learn more about Elle James at www.ellejames.com

Website | Facebook | Twitter | GoodReads | Newsletter | BookBub | Amazon

Or visit her alter ego Myla Jackson at mylajackson.com
Website | Facebook | Twitter | Newsletter

Follow Me!
www.ellejames.com
ellejamesauthor@gmail.com

ALSO BY ELLE JAMES

Bayou Brotherhood Protectors

Remy (#1)

Gerard (#2)

Lucas (#3)

Beau (#4)

Rafael (#5)

Valentin (#6)

Landry (#7)

Simon (#8)

Maurice (#9)

Jacques (#10)

Brotherhood Protectors Yellowstone

Saving Kyla (#1)

Saving Chelsea (#2)

Saving Amanda (#3)

Saving Liliana (#4)

Saving Breely (#5)

Saving Savvie (#6)

Saving Jenna (#7)

Saving Peyton (#8)

Saving Londyn (#9)

Brotherhood Protectors Colorado

SEAL Salvation (#1)

Total Meltdown (#7)

Take No Prisoners Series

SEAL's Honor (#1)

SEAL'S Desire (#2)

SEAL's Embrace (#3)

SEAL's Obsession (#4)

SEAL's Proposal (#5)

SEAL's Seduction (#6)

SEAL'S Defiance (#7)

SEAL's Deception (#8)

SEAL's Deliverance (#9)

SEAL's Ultimate Challenge (#10)

Texas Billionaire Club

Tarzan & Janine (#1)

Something To Talk About (#2)

Who's Your Daddy (#3)

Love & War (#4)

Billionaire Online Dating Service

The Billionaire Husband Test (#1)

The Billionaire Cinderella Test (#2)

The Billionaire Bride Test (#3)

The Billionaire Daddy Test (#4)

The Billionaire Matchmaker Test (#5)

The Billionaire Glitch Date (#6)

The Billionaire Perfect Date (#7)

The Billionaire Replacement Date (#8)

The Billionaire Wedding Date (#9)

Cajun Magic Mystery Series

Voodoo on the Bayou (#1)

Voodoo for Two (#2)

Deja Voodoo (#3)

Damned if You Voodoo (#4)

Voodoo or Die (#5)

The Outriders

Homicide at Whiskey Gulch (#1)

Hideout at Whiskey Gulch (#2)

Held Hostage at Whiskey Gulch (#3)

Setup at Whiskey Gulch (#4)

Missing Witness at Whiskey Gulch (#5)

Cowboy Justice at Whiskey Gulch (#6)

Boys Behaving Badly Anthologies

Rogues (#1)

Blue Collar (#2)

Pirates (#3)

Stranded (#4)

First Responder (#5)

Cowboys (#6)

Silver Soldiers (#7)

Secret Identities (#8)

Warrior's Conquest

Enslaved by the Viking Short Story

Conquests

Smokin' Hot Firemen

Protecting the Colton Bride

Protecting the Colton Bride & Colton's Cowboy Code

Heir to Murder

Secret Service Rescue

High Octane Heroes

Haunted

Engaged with the Boss

Cowboy Brigade

An Unexpected Clue

Under Suspicion, With Child

Texas-Size Secrets

Made in United States
Cleveland, OH
18 December 2024

12156876R00164